HARLEQUIN®
Presents

Harlequin Presents never fails to bring you the most gorgeous, brooding alpha heroes—so don't miss out on this month's irresistible collection!

THE ROYAL HOUSE OF NIROLI series continues with Susan Stephens's *Expecting His Royal Baby*. The king has found provocative prince Nico Fierezza a suitable bride. But Carrie has been in love with Nico—her boss—for years, and after one night of passion is pregnant!

When handsome Peter Ramsey discovers Erin's having his baby in *The Billionaire's Captive Bride* by Emma Darcy, he offers her the only thing he can think of to guarantee his child's security—marriage! In *The Greek Tycoon's Unwilling Wife* by Kate Walker, Andreas has lost his memory, but what will happen when he recalls throwing Rebecca out of his house on their wedding day—for reasons only he knows? If you're feeling festive, you'll love *The Boss's Christmas Baby* by Trish Morey, where a boss discovers his convenient mistress is expecting his baby. In *The Spanish Duke's Virgin Bride* by Chantelle Shaw, ruthless Spanish billionaire Duke Javier Herrera sees in Grace an opportunity for revenge *and* a contract wife! In *The Italian's Pregnant Mistress* by Cathy Williams, millionaire Angelo Falcone has Francesca in his power and in his bed, and this time he won't let her go. In *Contracted: A Wife for the Bedroom* by Carol Marinelli, Lily knows Hunter's ring will only be on her finger for twelve months, but soon a year doesn't seem long enough! Finally, brand-new author Susanne James brings you *Jed Hunter's Reluctant Bride,* where Jed demands Cryssie marry him because it makes good business sense, but Cryssie's feelings run deeper…. Enjoy!

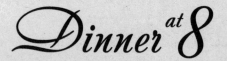

Dinner ^{at} *8*

Don't be late!

He's suave and sophisticated.

He's undeniably charming.

And above all, he treats her like a lady….

But beneath the tux, there's a primal, passionate
lover who's determined to make her his!

Wined, dined and swept away by a
British billionaire!

Susanne James

JED HUNTER'S RELUCTANT BRIDE

Dinner at 8

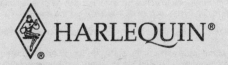

HARLEQUIN®

TORONTO • NEW YORK • LONDON
AMSTERDAM • PARIS • SYDNEY • HAMBURG
STOCKHOLM • ATHENS • TOKYO • MILAN • MADRID
PRAGUE • WARSAW • BUDAPEST • AUCKLAND

ISBN-13: 978-0-373-12682-8
ISBN-10:   0-373-12682-4

JED HUNTER'S RELUCTANT BRIDE

First North American Publication 2007.

Copyright © 2007 by Susanne James.

www.eHarlequin.com

Printed in U.S.A.

All about the author…
Susanne James

SUSANNE JAMES was born in Bristol, England,
of Welsh parentage. She has enjoyed creative
writing since childhood, completing her first—
sadly unpublished—novel at the age of twelve.
She has three grown-up children who were, and
are, her pride and joy, and who all live happily in
Oxfordshire with their families. Susanne was always
content to put the needs of the family before her
ambition to write seriously. However, along the
way, some published articles and short stories for
magazines and newspapers helped to keep the
dream alive. *Jed Hunter's Reluctant Bride* is her
first novel for Harlequin Presents.

A lyric coloratura soprano, Susanne is a classically
trained singer and has taken all the leading roles in
Gilbert and Sullivan operettas and major oratorios,
winning many awards in competitive festivals.
She currently sings with an opera group and her
ambitious, dedicated church choir, which gives her
constant inspiration and sometimes consolation
when her pen refuses to write. She recently
produced a CD featuring well-loved songs and arias,
from Handel to Gershwin.

Her big regret is that her beloved husband is no
longer here to share the pleasure of her recent
success. Susanne currently shares her life with
Toffee, her young Cavalier King Charles spaniel, who
decides when it's time to get up (early) and when a
walk in the park is overdue!

Susanne now lives in Somerset.

CHAPTER ONE

CRYSSIE TORE UP THE final flight of stairs which led to the toy department on the top floor of the large store. She'd spotted a queue of people waiting for the lift, so, with her slight frame and the flat, sensible shoes she always wore, she thought she'd beat them all to it, use her feet, and get there first!

Christmas Eve…the usual frantic nightmare, she thought ruefully. This was her final chance to do the rest of her shopping and, at last, to get what she'd come for. She'd rung earlier to make sure they had some of the much sought-after *Runaway Rascals*—dolls based on children's TV characters that Milo, her four-year-old nephew, adored. He never missed the programme, which featured the Rascals, and he desperately wanted one of them for himself. And Cryssie would do her utmost to get it for him. It had been out of stock everywhere for some time—surprise, surprise—but she knew that Latimer's had received a delivery yesterday, and she prayed that they hadn't all been snapped up.

Weaving her way frantically among the dozens of last-minute shoppers, she arrived at the appropriate counter and ran her eye quickly along the shelves. Yes! There were four there, on the top, grinning out from their cellophane-fronted boxes, and she heaved a sigh of relief. At last she'd made it!

Deftly, she was able to sneak in past the two or three customers there who were casually examining some other merchandise, and was already framing her request when out of nowhere a masculine voice spoke imperiously.

'Yes…thanks…I'll take the four.' And, after a pause, 'Put them on the account.'

'Certainly, Mr Hunter,' the assistant murmured, lowering her eyes coquettishly.

Cryssie stopped, open-mouthed in utter amazement, and a genuine feeling of desperation swept over her as the girl began to remove the boxes from the shelf and place them, one by one, on the counter in front of her. In her haste and anxiety Cryssie had not even noticed the man, who must have been standing there all the time, right beside her—and who had staked his claim in no uncertain terms! She stared up at the owner of that commanding voice, having to tilt her head back to take in this tall and pushy individual who'd got in before her.

He was an obvious business type, dressed in a sharp suit and immaculate shirt and tie, and from his lofty height had the distinct advantage over her five foot three. His richly dark hair fell carelessly around his ears, enhancing the line of his firm jaw…and his eyes! Black and glittering in their pools of startling white. They were calculating, even dangerous eyes, Cryssie thought instinctively.

Clearing her throat, she spoke to the assistant, her voice ringing out with all the authority she could manage. 'I hope those aren't the only ones—the *only* Runaway Rascals you've got there,' she said hotly. 'I only want *one*,' she added, as if to imply that anyone wanting four was greedy and thoughtless!

The girl glanced briefly at Cryssie. 'I'm sorry,' she said, as she wedged the boxes into two large carrier bags. 'These actually are the last. We've never known such a manic demand for *anything*, and—'

'But I rang this morning and you promised…you *assured* me you had plenty,' Cryssie protested.

'We did—and they've all gone…like hot cakes! And the management decided that we weren't to reserve any over the phone—as I told you when we spoke. First come, first served seemed fairest.' She finished packing, and pushed the bags across the counter. 'We will be getting a delivery at the end of January,' she added helpfully. 'Not that that's much good now, of course. You can leave your address and phone number with us for when the dolls are next in, but you'll have to explain that the Runaway Rascals have all run away from Santa's sleigh!'

Oh, very funny, Cryssie thought angrily. She glared up at the man, who glanced back down at her casually and without apparent interest. As if she didn't exist—as if he couldn't care less about what anyone *else* wanted! He could at least have made *some* sort of apology, she thought.

Then, with one lean and sunburnt hand, he took hold of the bags and turned to go. Not apparently even having to sign anything, or produce any cash, Cryssie noticed. That somehow made it worse, because the dolls were terribly expensive for what they were. She was the only consistent earner in their household, and had learned to be thrifty and save for things like Christmas and birthdays. She wouldn't have *dared* have an account at Latimer's, or anywhere else for that matter. Pay as you go was the safest, she'd always been taught.

As they both moved away from the counter he hesitated and looked down at her properly at last. 'That was…unfortunate,' he drawled. 'The ordering department obviously got it wrong this time, didn't they… Or perhaps we should all shop earlier?' he added pointedly. And, with a barely perceptible tilt of his arrogant mouth, he turned abruptly and walked away, leaving Cryssie standing there feeling utterly defeated.

So…she shouldn't have left it until the last minute, should she? But then—so had he! Except that he'd arrived at the store just a few seconds before her!

She looked around vaguely for a minute or two, wondering what to do next. She knew Milo would be so disappointed to wake up and not find the precious toy in his stocking. It was true there would be plenty of other gifts to unwrap—but this was the one he really wanted, and had been keeping on about for months.

Her face still flushed with annoyance, she picked up a pair of football boots, examining them for size and wondering whether she should buy them. Milo was football mad, and hadn't yet had a proper pair, always kicking around in his trainers—which were expensive enough, heaven only knew. Maybe these, together with a new ball, would ease his disappointment.

Cryssie leaned against a counter for a minute, feeling stressed and irritated. At the age of twenty-five, she sometimes felt the responsibilities that life had placed on her were almost too much to put up with. Since the death of their parents ten years earlier in a car accident, she and her sister Polly— younger by two years—had lived with Great-Aunt Josie, until she, too, had died. Luckily that had been before they'd known that Polly was expecting Milo, or that the man in question had done a convenient runner. So now the two women and the little boy lived in a small rented terraced house in the town, with Cryssie the only one bringing in any real money.

After a few minutes she began to calm down, accepting ruefully that the self-satisfied owner of the four dolls obviously had four kids, and it would be no good giving to three and the fourth going without. A soft voice by her side made her turn around to see the assistant standing there, obviously concerned.

'Are you okay?' the woman enquired. 'You look shattered…'

'Oh, I'm fine,' Cryssie said forlornly. 'Just tired…'

'Tell me about it.' The assistant paused. 'I'm really sorry about just now—but there wasn't anything I could do. I'd have loved to keep a doll back for you, because I know how many times you've been in asking for one. Look, do leave your address and phone number with us.'

'All right,' Cryssie replied, and gave the girl her details. 'Not your fault. I just hope that man's little darlings are made to appreciate their good luck.'

'He hasn't got any little darlings…he's not married.' The assistant lowered her voice. 'Didn't you realise who that was?'

Cryssie shrugged. 'No…should I?'

'Oh, I thought everyone knew him… That was Jeremy—or Jed—Hunter. The *boss* of this place,' she emphasised, as if announcing royalty.

Cryssie knew that Latimer's was owned by the Hunter family, but wasn't acquainted with any of them, or with what they looked like. She certainly hadn't ever seen *him* before. If she had, she would have remembered!

'Up until a year or so ago we never saw him,' the girl went on, 'but he seems to have taken over from his parents—who are getting on, obviously.' She stifled a yawn. 'Some of the staff are a bit afraid of him—he can be stroppy if things don't go right. Not that *I'm* afraid,' she added defensively. 'I mean, he's always courteous…but rather demanding, with a bit of a short fuse at times. Still, I suppose anyone that drop-dead gorgeous *and* rich can afford to be moody when he feels like it.'

'I suppose so,' Cryssie agreed dismissively, not particularly wanting to join in a chorus of admiration for this Mr Jed

Hunter—not the way she was feeling at the moment! But he certainly seemed to be the man who had everything…including the one and only thing she—or Milo—wanted. And there was no way they'd be getting it now. The eleventh hour had come and gone.

'Anyway, I've got your name and details,' the assistant said. 'And as soon as we get more stock I'll contact you.'

'Oh, fine,' Cryssie said dully, beginning to wish that the Runaway Rascals had never been thought of! 'Anyway, if he hasn't got any children, what did he want them for?' she blurted out, picking up the football boots.

'Couldn't tell you,' the assistant said, turning to go back to her counter. She hesitated. 'Do you have other children to buy for as well?'

'No—and I don't have any of my own,' Cryssie replied. 'We're just the three of us…my sister and her little boy—my nephew, Milo—and me. But I'm the one who has to do all the chasing about, I'm afraid.' Cryssie's shoulders drooped for a second. 'My sister isn't…well,' she added quietly, wondering why she was bothering to air her problems in public.

'Oh, dear…and does she—can she—work?' the woman asked gently.

'Occasionally—on a part-time basis,' Cryssie replied. 'She trained as a beauty consultant.'

'Oh…that's nice…' The assistant glanced at Cryssie curiously—and Cryssie knew instinctively what she was thinking! Why doesn't your sister give *you* a makeover? Because Cryssie's small-framed, insignificant appearance was not the sort to turn heads. Polly was the beauty of the family, with her willowy figure, rich auburn hair and large grey eyes.

'And do you work full time?' the assistant enquired, obviously glad of a few moments' opportunity to chat.

'Yes—I'm employed at Hydebound. Been there three years now.'

'Oh, I know them,' the woman said at once. 'I was given one of their fantastic handbags for my birthday. Beautifully made, isn't it, all their stuff? A bit expensive, but well worth the cost!'

Cryssie smiled, genuinely pleased to hear that. 'Of course we're only a very small, independent firm,' she said. 'Not like this place!'

She waited her turn to purchase the football boots and the ball, and started making for the stairs when the delicious smell of coffee drifted out from the nearby restaurant area. She hesitated, realising that she hadn't eaten a thing since her cheese sandwich at lunchtime. No one at work had even had time to make a cup of tea that day. She glanced at her watch, her sudden desire for a long, hot injection of caffeine becoming irresistible. Anyway, perhaps if she sat there for a while most of the home-going traffic would have subsided.

There were still plenty of people taking advantage of a sit-down and a drink, and Cryssie plonked her bags down by a table for two in the corner. Then, going over to pick up a tray, she slid it along the counter, unable to stop herself choosing a sugary doughnut as well. She knew it would be ages before she got around to making supper, and Polly wouldn't have done anything towards it.

She poured herself a large mug of coffee, and placed it on the tray, then moved towards the till. And from out of nowhere a deep voice—*that* deep voice interrupted her thoughts. 'Allow me,' he said smoothly.

'Pardon?' Cryssie twisted around in confusion, and stared once more into the face of the man she now knew to be the owner of the store. 'I'm sorry, I…'

'Allow me to pay for your drink,' he repeated slowly, as if

making himself clear to a backward child. 'It's the least I can do,' he added.

To her intense annoyance Cryssie felt the colour rising unstoppably in her child-like face. 'Please—don't feel—*obliged*—to do anything,' she said, her voice cool despite her sudden rise in body temperature.

'Oh, I don't feel obliged, exactly,' he replied, equally coolly, 'but it would give me…pleasure…to settle your bill.'

'Well, I can't think why—' Cryssie began, but he interrupted her.

'Because of what happened earlier,' he said, transfixing her with his impenetrable gaze. 'I'm sorry that you weren't able to purchase what you wanted just now.'

'Oh, well, I… It doesn't matter…' she began—though it *did* matter. It mattered a lot. But at this precise moment it didn't matter which one of them paid for her coffee, just so long as she could get it down her—and soon!

She indicated the table where her things were and, placing his own drink beside hers on the tray, he followed her across the room. They sat down, and he passed her the plate with the doughnut and set their coffees down. She noticed that the carrier bags with *his* shopping were nowhere to be seen… He'd probably off-loaded them on to one of his underlings to take care of!

She began to feel strangely self-conscious, sitting so close to this undeniably handsome man—so close that it was difficult for their knees not to touch beneath the small table! Not that his obvious heart-throb appeal was of the least interest to *her*, she told herself. That part of her life was in a state of permanent shut-down!

Now, she picked up her coffee and forced herself to meet Jed Hunter's gaze over the rim of the mug. Of course, she reassured herself, these panicky feelings running through her were due to the fact that she was sitting in close—very close—proximity to the vastly wealthy owner of the store. He would naturally be a powerful member of the community—but what the hell? So what? *She* was one of his valued customers, and without people like her coming regularly through the doors he wouldn't be able to afford his undoubtedly lavish life-style! So she should calm down, she told herself sternly.

He looked at her steadily while she put a piece of doughnut into her mouth. 'What do you think of those…are they good?' he enquired casually.

Cryssie swallowed before answering, dabbing some sugar from her lips. 'This one's not bad,' she said coolly, 'but the quality of the cakes and pastries here can be patchy. I've had some pretty dire ones in the past—most of them frozen, I suppose. You'd think a reputable store like this would cook them on the premises and serve them fresh, wouldn't you? A trained *monkey* could dunk a doughnut.' She took another bite and looked across at him again. 'Would you like to try a bit?' she asked, knowing full well what his answer would be! He was not likely to lower his prestige by sinking his teeth into a sticky bun! Certainly not sitting with someone like her!

Tilting his mouth slightly at one corner, he said, 'No… thank you. I wouldn't dream of depriving you.' He paused. 'There's so little of you, you look as if you really need a square meal rather than a quick fix.'

Cryssie shot him one of the cold looks she knew she was capable of. What a colossal nerve! She knew she must look pale and tired—and who wouldn't with the weeks *they'd* had recently?—but she didn't like it pointed out! And certainly not by this complete stranger. Because that was what he was, after all.

'Well, it'll be some time before I have the pleasure of enjoying my "square meal",' she said icily, 'because I still have to collect the poultry from the butcher before he closes on my way home, then make the stuffing and do the vegetables so that we can enjoy my...Milo...in the morning. See him open up his stocking.'

'Ah—Milo...' He drank from his mug of black unsweetened coffee. 'So it was Milo you wanted the toy for?'

'Yes,' she said briefly. 'He'll be five soon.' Then her earlier frustration threatened to surface again. 'It seems to me that Latimer's have got it well and truly wrong this time. They clearly didn't have the vision to see that demand would exceed the supply they were prepared to buy for their shelves. I mean...this is the biggest store for *miles* around—not some little corner shop with limited cashflow!'

'If, on the other hand, supply had exceeded demand, or this craze had fallen off suddenly,' he intervened, 'they'd have perhaps a hundred cases of Runaway Rascals to sell off at a cut price in the sale...and there goes their profit.'

'Their *profit!*' Cryssie nearly exploded. 'This place must be awash with profit! They can afford to share a bit of it, for heaven's sake, rather than let small children down at Christmas!'

The hint of a smile played around his lips as he listened to her outburst, and he stared at her for a moment. She was devoid of any make-up, he noticed, but wasn't an altogether unattractive woman—though her outfit of a rather shapeless fawn jacket over a brown skirt was hardly the height of fashion. Her long fair hair was drawn fiercely back behind her ears, accentuating a smooth, high forehead, and her green eyes, looking at him squarely, dominated her oval-shaped face. Her only jewellery appeared to be a tiny pair of gold ear studs. An honest description of her would be 'wholesome', he decided briefly. His lips curled slightly as he found himself assessing her. Well, that was what he always did when meeting a member of the opposite sex, wasn't it? Took stock, so to speak. And this one would be placed in the 'unmemorable' category, he decided.

Cryssie finished her coffee, waiting for him to take her up on her last remark, but he said no more. And whether it was the sudden effect of caffeine and sugar in her bloodstream, or because she couldn't have cared less if she insulted the owner of Latimer's sitting next to her, she threw discretion to the winds and sailed on blindly.

'There are all sorts of ways they could tighten up in this place,' she said. 'Generally, I mean. For example, they often don't seem to stock the same things twice…it's so annoying!' She wasn't going to enlighten him as to what she was talking about—a particularly pretty bra and pants set she'd bought for Polly, which had never been repeated. 'And as for getting a member of staff to help you –they're invisible, or looking the other way! It encourages shoplifting with so few assistants around. I'm sure anyone could help themselves to anything they fancied and march out without paying. No one would notice!'

Her eyes sparkled with ocean-green intensity in the artificial light of the restaurant, and without giving him a chance to get a word in, she went on. 'I work for Hydebound—do you know it? We deal exclusively in leather goods, all made by local experts, and—'

'Yes…I do know of them,' he murmured. 'They're right on the outskirts of town…rather out of the way, aren't they?'

Cryssie nodded. 'Our handbags, belts and briefcases are always in demand, and everyone takes responsibility for what they do. As with all smaller concerns, we do have our problems from time to time, but then everyone works all the harder.'

She sat back defiantly, and was suddenly aware of his eyes softening briefly with mild amusement as he looked across at her.

'Well, you obviously have very firm opinions,' he said. 'And by the sound of it Hydebound are very lucky to have you on their staff.'

Cryssie bit her lip for a second, anxious thoughts suddenly clouding her expression. Hydebound, like all small businesses, could be commercially vulnerable at times. Although they had a great reputation for quality and design, the price of leather and the regular increase in running costs, not to mention competition from much cheaper imports from all the new EC countries, regularly gave cause for concern. A detectable shiver ran through her, and she suddenly wished that she was home now, sitting comfortably in front of the fire.

'I really have to go,' she said abruptly, standing up, and he stood as well, moving her chair back for her as she picked up her bags. 'Thanks for the coffee—and the doughnut,' she added airily.

'I expect you're looking forward to a good holiday… Do you work full time?' he asked casually.

'I do,' Cryssie said, shooting him a glance. He probably didn't approve of that, she thought… Mothers working full time instead of staying at home, looking after the family. He looked that type. Well, he could think what he liked, and she wasn't going to enlighten him about her true personal situation—that she wasn't Milo's mother. It was none of his business.

He smiled for the first time. 'I hope you and the family… and Milo…have a great Christmas,' he said.

She turned to go. 'Thanks,' she said quickly, as she brushed past him. Well, he might be the man with everything, she thought, trying not to feel cross all over again, but the only thing of his *she* wanted was one of those wretched dolls!

That was the last thing she'd have expected to happen to her on Christmas Eve, she thought, as the lift sped down through the floors. Telling the owner of Latimer's what she thought of his store! To be honest, she *had* laid it on a bit thick, she acknowledged, because she really did enjoy shopping there, despite all her remarks. But saying all she had had sort of helped ease her annoyance. She glanced down at the bag holding the boots and the ball... She hoped they'd be sufficient compensation—though she doubted it!

Jeremy Hunter watched her go as she swiftly walked away from him, a strange expression on his handsome face. He'd met many women—too many women—in his life—but no one quite like *that!* A feisty female, yet a vulnerable woman. As she'd warmed to what she was saying she'd positively glowed, a rosy blush colouring her cheeks, lighting up her face. He shrugged inwardly, then turned to go. He'd stayed around longer than he'd intended, and he still had these blasted toys to deliver!

Jeremy—or Jed, as he was known to everyone except his parents—steered his silver Porsche effortlessly through the traffic, wishing that he was going back to his flat in London rather than to the family pile in the country. But it was unthinkable that he wouldn't spend Christmas with his parents, Henry and Alice, who doted on their son. Their only son. Whose one great failing in their eyes was his choice in women!

'When are you going to find yourself a proper woman?' his father would regularly complain. 'A woman with something between her ears for a change. Never mind where her other attributes might lie!' Henry Hunter was an outspoken man.

Jed admitted to himself that he *had* been susceptible where the opposite sex was concerned. It was hard not to be when women fell at his feet, offering themselves to him with seldom any shame or reticence—and he'd loved it! He owned up to that. But it was different now. He'd made one really big, bad mistake, and he'd learned from it. Well, at thirty-six years old it was about time he grew up!

The traffic was thinning now, and he was able to increase his speed towards the parental home and the festive meal that Megan, the housekeeper, would have ready for them. The family would sit down together, the three of them at the huge oval table, and talk. Discuss business, balance sheets, the state of the economy…

He'd wished many times in his life that he had siblings to share the pressure of being the sole beneficiary of all his parents' love and affection. Could too much be worse than too little? he asked himself—then felt bad about thinking it. He realised that he'd had more than his fair share of all the good things in life…a privileged education, and travel to all corners of the world, with never a thought that the money could, or would, ever dry up. And until the last couple of years he hadn't even been expected to have any hands-on input in the family businesses—the two other Latimer's stores in the Midlands, and two country house hotels in Wales. Settling down to the dreary business of a structured and demanding lifestyle had been proving difficult for Jed, but he had eventually—and willingly—taken up the reins. His parents were no longer in their prime, and Henry had been having a few health problems.

As he waited at traffic lights, his thoughts kept returning to that woman—strange little thing, he mused, not at all conscious of herself as female in the usual sense. No lowering her eyes or fluttering her lashes, no fiddling with her hair. The sort of reaction he usually got. Her eyes—quite pretty, actually—had seldom looked away from his when she was speaking. He wondered briefly what sort of a man she slept with—who Milo's father was, what he was like. He hoped he could stand up for himself! He imagined her now, going home with all that shopping, going home to her husband and child, to catch up on all the household chores... She'd said she worked full time, so it would be all there waiting for her, even on Christmas Eve.

She was certainly no seductress—he was expert at recognising *that* brand of female! Though she probably had her own powers of persuasion hidden somewhere, he thought wryly, a brief smile touching his lips as he remembered her sparky comments about the shop. He shifted in his seat, irritated by his own thoughts, irritated that a casual encounter with a completely insignificant woman was exercising his concentration. Then he frowned. He'd remember what she'd said about the shop, though—if anything could improve the running of the place then it was up to him to see that it was done.

CHAPTER TWO

CRYSSIE let herself out of the house silently, so as not to disturb Polly and Milo, who were still fast asleep. It was New Year's Eve and not yet seven-thirty a.m., but the Lewis brothers, who owned Hydebound, had called a meeting for the staff. Cryssie frowned as she drove along in her ancient banger of a car wondering why this early, and what it could all be about.

Thinking back over Christmas, she smiled happily to herself. Despite Polly not eating much of all the delicious festive food, Milo had had a wonderful time with all his new toys—and especially with his very own Runaway Rascal! Because, unbelievably, quite late on Christmas Eve, the doorbell had rung and the Latimer's assistant she'd dealt with earlier had stood outside, clutching a bag containing one of the dolls.

'You'll never believe it,' the girl had said, 'but we found one in the stockroom. It had fallen down and got lodged behind some boxes. Better late than never, eh?'

Cryssie had been almost dumbstruck with delight, and full of gratitude that the assistant had bothered to bring it.

'No problem—your house is on my way home,' the woman had assured her.

She wished she could show Mr High and Mighty that he wasn't the only one who always got his own way! But she must be careful what she spent for a bit… She had always been frightened of getting into debt, and sometimes lay awake worrying what would happen to all of them—to Milo—if the unthinkable happened and she was no longer able to support the family. That the little boy should ever have to be fostered, or looked after by someone else, was the stuff of nightmares!

When she arrived, Robert and Neil Lewis, the owners of Hydebound, were already at their desks. Neither of them smiled as she came in, but merely nodded, and her heart sank. They weren't happy, she thought, and by the time the rest of the staff arrived the air of gloom had deepened. This could only mean one thing, Cryssie thought ruefully—disappointing financial news, even though recent sales had been so good. Well, they'd survived those times before, and would again! Anyway, the rather elderly brothers always tended to look on the black side!

Robert came swiftly to the point. 'We're very sorry to inform you all that the company is in some difficulty,' he said soberly. 'The banks have called in our loans, and we can't continue living on credit any longer.'

A stunned silence greeted his words. 'You've all been aware how things have been for some time, but it has come to the point where we can no longer pay our bills.'

Cryssie swallowed, feeling a tightening in her chest as she took in the news.

'My brother and I have come to the conclusion that we shall have to discontinue trading. Despite all our efforts, events have overtaken us.' For an awful moment the old man looked as if he was about to cry!

Cryssie's knees started to shake. This was terrible—for all of them! It could be weeks, months, before they found other suitable employment. Jobs in this town didn't grow on trees!

And what about the men and women in the workroom who'd been there for years and years? What chance would *they* have of starting afresh somewhere else? It took just a few seconds for all these thoughts to buzz around in her mind, like angry bees, and the knot of anxiety in her stomach grew rapidly into a huge ball of tangible fear.

Neil Lewis took up the story. 'However, we've been approached by some interested buyers. They came unexpectedly some weeks ago, and it was an offer we couldn't refuse.' He looked around him steadily. 'The new owners apparently intend letting things run as they are—for the moment. So your jobs are secure—for the time being, at least.' He took a sip of water from the glass in front of him. 'Your new employers will be here in a few minutes. They're coming here to meet you all.'

Cryssie stared down at her clenched fists, trying to take in what had just been said and how it was going to affect *her*. Who could tell what was going to happen? Who would be made redundant? These new owners would undoubtedly make sweeping alterations...perhaps make her own position no longer 'necessary'... Her degree course had taught her how common it was for takeovers to happen overnight, for staff to find themselves jobless. And that there was no legal requirement for them to be found other employment, or be given more than minimum financial redress. This small and cosy world would change overnight. It was inevitable.

An internal phone shrilled suddenly, and Robert stood up. 'That's to tell me they're downstairs,' he said.

He left the room, and in the ensuing silence everyone shifted in their seats, no one uttering a word. Well, what was there to say?

In a couple of minutes the door opened and Robert came back in, followed by the new owner of Hydebound. Everyone stood up rather awkwardly to greet him—Cryssie having to grip the arm of her chair to steady herself, her heart jumping into her throat and the colour sweeping over her cheeks like an unstoppable incoming tide.

'Let me introduce Mr Jeremy Hunter,' Robert said quietly, 'who, together with his parents, owns Latimer's store in the town.' He paused. 'So you will be in very safe hands, I'm sure.'

By this time Cryssie's mouth was so dry she thought she would choke! That she and Jeremy Hunter were to meet again like this, and in these circumstances, was something she would never have dreamed of in a million years!

He was formally dressed, as before, and in the revealing morning light he cut an imposing figure as he glanced around at each of them in turn, his dense black eyes seeming to penetrate the minds of everyone there.

Cryssie was the last to be introduced—which was just as well, because it gave her time to recover from the shocks of the last few moments. Her mind was doing somersaults! He caught her hand and held it for a few seconds in a strong grip, looking down at her, searing her mind with the intensity of his gaze. Cryssie could only guess what he was thinking, but it filled her with an indescribable sense of helplessness. The inscrutable expression on his face, his uncompromising mouth which remained unsmilingly set in a straight line, gave nothing away. But it made her feel like a small child on her first day at school!

After a moment, he said coldly, 'I believe *we* have already met, haven't we?' It was a rhetorical question, coldly put. Then he turned away dismissively, and Cryssie wished she could just disappear. Especially as she was conscious of others' curious glances.

Although his remark couldn't be described as a put-down,

it hadn't exactly been filled with the warmth of recognition, either! Well, after all she'd said about Latimer's, was that a surprise? She cringed at the memory. If there were to be any sackings, she'd be the first to go!

Jeremy Hunter only stayed for half an hour, apologising that his parents were away, so could not be there to speak to them. When he and the Lewis brothers had gone downstairs, everyone started talking at once.

'I find it hard to believe,' Rose, the secretary, said at last. 'We've all known things have been difficult, but I never thought the Lewises would throw in the towel.' She turned to Cryssie. 'He said you knew each other. How come?'

Cryssie coloured up, and said hastily, 'Oh, we don't *know* each other at all! We sort of bumped into each other in his store.' She paused. 'I'm afraid I said some rude things about Latimer's, which he's not likely to forget or forgive. So I might as well hand in *my* notice now!'

At five-thirty that day, Cryssie was one of the last to leave the building, and she made her way across the dimly lit deserted car park where she always left her vehicle. She couldn't wait to get home, to hug Milo and give him his tea, then bath him and put him to bed. All the things that made her feel happy and contented. She knew that her news wouldn't have much impact on her sister, who didn't seem to think about anyone or anything but her own problems.

She was just about to get into her car when a footstep in the darkness nearly made her jump out of her skin.

'Sorry,' Jed Hunter said. 'I didn't mean to alarm you.'

She swung around and looked up to face him, only just able to make out his features in the dim light. But his eyes were visible enough, and they bored into her inescapably.

'Oh, I—' she began, but he interrupted her.

'I realise that you may have been…surprised…at this morning's news,' he said, 'but I had specifically asked that no names were mentioned until I arrived.' He paused. 'It was obviously a shock, but sometimes there's no easy way to deliver news of the sort you've all had—though I sincerely hope that this change in circumstances may prove to be not that bad in the long run.' His words were spoken with a calculating directness. He was a businessman, and there was not much sentiment in business. Cryssie was well aware of that!

'Well, that rather depends on you and your future plans for Hydebound,' Cryssie said, swallowing hard and trying to display a coolness she was far from feeling—and wishing for some unaccountable reason that she wasn't wearing the same fawn jacket she'd been wearing on Christmas Eve!

She'd never been much interested in fashion, nor did she have Polly's dress sense. Whereas her new boss obviously took pains with *his* appearance. She was acutely conscious of the familiar scent of expensive leather from the loose, casual jacket he had on, carelessly opened to reveal the front of his gleaming shirt. By now her eyes had become more accustomed to her surroundings, and she could see that he had discarded his tie, exposing a strong, tanned neck.

He shrugged. 'I thought I'd made it clear that it will be business as usual for now,' he said smoothly.

He continued staring down at her, and for once Cryssie was tongue-tied! She kept remembering how she'd gone on—not only about Latimer's, but about Hydebound, and what a good company she worked for…all the time not realising that the man intended buying them out! His little secret, she thought—and it might even have been *her* words which had convinced him that he was purchasing a good investment!

'Well,' Cryssie said eventually, 'I'm sure you will be able to rely on the staff to continue working as we always have done. Loyally, and to the best of our ability.'

'Oh, I'm counting on it,' he said, and the perceptible jutting of his jaw as he uttered the words sent a small shiver down Cryssie's spine.

He was not likely to be swayed by any emotional feelings where the firm was concerned, she thought. It would be business—and strictly hard-headed business at that. The assistant at Latimer's had made it only too clear that he was someone who expected to get his own way and run things exactly as *he* wanted. And it had to be admitted that the Lewis brothers had not exactly moved with the times during the forty-odd years they had owned the company. In fact, its time-warp atmosphere was part of its charm—everyone said so.

She was about to get into her car when he moved forward, stopping her for a moment.

'I do have a favour to ask,' he said slowly. 'The Lewises have given me a pretty comprehensive idea of what I'm buying, but I'd appreciate a meeting with you—one-to-one— to get to the grass roots and hear things from another angle.'

Cryssie looked up into his face for a moment, trying to read what was behind the expression in those deep coal-black eyes. She hoped he wasn't anticipating that she'd give away any family secrets, or express a personal opinion about her colleagues. If he thought that he might learn something from her that the Lewises had deliberately not told him, he'd better think again!

'Of course I can attend a meeting,' she said rather primly, in answer to his request. 'We all have tomorrow off—New Year's Day—but I'll be at my desk the day after. It *is* work as usual then, isn't it?' she asked demurely.

'Of course,' he said. 'But I was thinking more on the lines of dinner somewhere. I always think that a relaxed meal and a glass or two of good wine brings out the best in most situations.'

He paused, and Cryssie felt her whole body tremble. She hadn't expected a *dinner* invitation—or *any* invitation—from her new boss, especially remembering their earlier acquaintance! How acutely embarrassing—and what on earth would her colleagues think when they found out? Especially Rose, who always seemed a bit jealous of Cryssie.

'But how thoughtless of me,' he continued. 'New Year's Eve is a time for couples, isn't it? I'm sure you have somewhere special lined up for tonight.'

She stared up at him blankly. 'What...you mean... *tonight?*' she exclaimed in amazement. Surely he was inundated with invitations to glitzy parties? This particular night of the year was hardly the time to take an unimportant employee out—for a *meeting!*

'Certainly tonight,' he said implacably. 'Unless, of course, you have better things to do. And there is Milo to consider... Would someone do the babysitting honours?'

Fancy him remembering Milo's name—that was at least one point in his favour! She looked up into that rugged, handsome face and smiled suddenly. It might be quite nice to go somewhere for dinner instead of always preparing it, she thought. 'Babysitting's never any problem, Mr Hunter,' she said. Then, deciding that there was no point in hedging, because he was sure to find out sooner or later, added, 'As a matter of fact I'm not married. I never have been.'

She stood there, challenging him to say something which would indicate what he thought about selfish unmarried mothers—women who thought they could have it all—because that was obviously what he *would* think.

But his expression gave nothing away, and he stood back to allow her to get into the car. 'Where do you live?' he asked abruptly. 'Will eight o'clock be too soon? I have a table booked at the Laurels for nine.'

Cryssie tried to stop her mouth opening and closing like a fish! The Laurels was the most expensive restaurant in the area—she'd never expected to step inside the place, let alone be treated to dinner! And in the same second she thought. So he's already booked a table! The man who always got everything he wanted! For a moment she thought she'd scupper his plans and refuse, for the sheer hell of it! Instead, she said, 'We live at number nine Birch End Lane—do you know it? Right by the public tennis courts.' Why *should* he know their humble address? she thought. His own would be somewhere magnificent, far away from here.

'I do know where it is,' he answered at once. 'I've played on those courts many times.'

She finally got into the car and closed the door, winding down the window and glancing up. 'Do you need me to fetch any papers or figures from the office for our discussion later?' she enquired pertly.

'That won't be necessary,' he said. 'I merely want a more general outline of how everything—everyone—ticks. I'm not looking for statistics.' He paused, then added casually, 'It's black tie this evening, by the way. One night in the year when they expect that sort of thing at the Laurels.'

Cryssie nodded as she started the car and prepared to reverse slowly. 'I'll be ready at eight,' she said airily through the open window. Then she pulled away and drove out into the rush-hour traffic, her mind in a complete and utter whirl!

The whole day had been surreal enough, she thought, from the morning's bombshell to the non-stop chattering and analysing of the situation, and finally being practically accosted by her new employer and invited out to dinner on New Year's Eve! And why *her*, for heaven's sake? But then, why *not* her? she asked herself. As he'd said, they had met before—were acquainted in a funny sort of way. He obviously thought it a sufficient enough opening that he could use for the purpose he'd said—to find out about his staff on a more personal level than he was likely to do through discussion with the Lewis brothers. Especially as she'd proved herself to be not backward in coming forward!

She kept thinking of all the things she'd said to him on Christmas Eve, trying to recall whether she'd been as off-hand and uncomplimentary as her memory now told her she had. One thing was certain—she was a marked woman… Her out-spokenness had made her stand out from the crowd, and not in an exactly flattering way!

As she contemplated the evening to come a sudden thought struck her, and she nearly swerved off the road in horror. What on earth did she have to wear? It was obvious that his mentioning he would be appearing in evening dress was to give her a clue as to what she should do about it herself. He probably thought that without some prompting, she'd turn up in jeans and a sweater! And the horrible fact was she didn't *have* anything to wear! She never went anywhere that made it necessary to buy pretty clothes, so normally it wasn't a problem. Her wardrobe consisted entirely of skirts, shirts, tops and denims. She wasn't *into* clothes. She left all that sort of stuff to Polly—even though her sister never went anywhere, either. And it was no use thinking that anything of Polly's would fit her, because there was a five inch difference in their height and she'd only trip up and fall headlong and embar-rass Jed Hunter even further!

Perhaps she could plead a sudden migraine and not go after all? she thought desperately—then realised she had no idea how to contact the man. She groaned, and had a terrible sinking feeling that this was going to be one of the worst nights of her life.

When she got home, Polly had already put Milo to bed, and was curled up on the sofa, reading.

'I've got to go out tonight, Poll,' Cryssie said casually, as she went into the kitchen with some shopping she'd collected.

'Where to?' her sister asked, without looking up.

'Oh, just a meeting—a work thing,' Cryssie said.

Presently, in her bedroom, she opened her wardrobe door and stared at the rather anonymous array of clothes—as if hoping that something suitable would magically appear. But she knew there was *nothing!* Panic set in, and she sat down silently, her head in her hands. She didn't *need* this!

Suddenly, her heel touched the edge of the large cardboard box holding the only 'occasion' dress she'd ever possessed. A deep ocean-green number she'd bought in a charity shop for her eighteenth birthday party, seven years ago. And after her A level results they'd all gone to the end-of-school bash, and everyone had dressed up. She had truthfully not given the dress a thought since that night… Could it possibly still fit her? And what would she look like in it after all this time?

Dragging the box out, she wiped the fine layer of dust from the lid with a tissue, then removed the garment and, standing up, shook out the folds, holding it against her and staring at herself in the mirror. Well, the colour was still good, and, being of a satin-type material, it hadn't attracted the attention of any moths, and the creases would press out okay. It had a simple boat-shaped neckline, and drop-waisted full skirt—which she knew was horribly old-fashioned—but that was just too bad. It was this or nothing. As for her feet, the best she could do was wear her flat brown summer sandals.

Heaving a sigh, she stepped into the dress and zipped it up at the back. Well, it still fitted—that was something. But, gazing at herself honestly, she realised how naïve and—well…boring, she appeared. Impulsively, she shook her hair out from the band that held it back in a knot, and thought…no! That made her look like Alice in Wonderland! Well, there was no point standing there agonising, she thought. By the time she'd showered and pressed the dress His Majesty would be arriving!

She stopped dead in her tracks for a second. Was all this *really* happening? she asked herself. The whole day was like a long, disturbing dream—and it wasn't over yet!

At precisely eight o'clock, a discreet tap on the door announced Jed Hunter's arrival, and Cryssie hastily let herself out of the house before Polly could show any interest. She smiled briefly up at him as they went down the rather cracked and untidy garden path together, pulling her jacket protectively around her against the bitter wind.

'I didn't ring the bell in case it woke Milo,' he said, as he handed her into the car.

'Thanks,' she answered, privately surprised that with no family of his own he should be that thoughtful. She nestled into the luxury of the soft leather seat, putting her head back and letting out a sigh of pleasure. This was living, she thought— even if it was probably the only time she'd experience it. She'd never even sat in a car like this, never mind felt herself floating along the tarmac so effortlessly—so *importantly!*

He glanced across at her as they gathered speed. 'Are you sure you don't mind about tonight?' he asked. 'About leaving your little boy with a minder, I mean?'

'Oh, my sister's there. She lives with us. He'll be fine,' she added, closing her eyes momentarily, feeling a bit like Cinderella being taken to the ball. Except that at this stage of the plot she wasn't supposed to be being escorted by Prince Charming—that should come much later! That, however hard she tried to think of this evening as a business date, the fact that she was sitting close—very close—to probably the most handsome man she'd ever set eyes on made it difficult for her not to want to enjoy herself. Even if she *did* find him annoying and imperious. She could not deny experiencing a frisson, a sensation, as any female would, and she was suddenly startled by a certain lustful intensity! This was something very new to her, and she must stifle it at once, she told herself fiercely. Wasn't he the sort of man she would never again allow herself to feel anything for at all—ever?

She shifted in her seat and he turned briefly to look across.

'Are you comfortable enough?' he asked. 'Is the seat in the correct position for you? I can lower or raise it for you…'

'No…no… That isn't necessary,' Cryssie said at once. 'It's fine, really.'

He turned back to stare straight ahead, and Cryssie, looking at him covertly, was painfully aware of his hands, of his long fingers curled around the steering wheel, the strength of his taut thighs beneath the fine fabric of his evening trousers. She swallowed, trying to get a grip on this unlooked-for situation…and on her own senses! She didn't want to feel this curious mix of excitement and trepidation. She just wanted to feel *normal!* There promised to be enough upheaval in her life with everything going on at work. As for him, *he* would certainly not have the slightest interest in her as a woman—that was the most obvious statement of the century! He could have his pick of the crop, and was still unmarried, clearly taking his time over deciding which lucky female would eventually bear his children. It was plain that tonight he was putting business before pleasure, asking this little Miss Nobody— with, as he thought, an illegitimate child—to accompany him on this night of all nights.

Cryssie smiled inwardly. All his lady-friends, waiting hopefully by the phone for that longed-for invitation, would be disappointed! He was too interested in finding out more about the business he'd just paid good money for. That was what this evening was all about! And who better to spill the beans, to tell any unofficial secrets, than the employee he had so recently had a conversation with—the one who had proved unafraid to speak out?

Presently, he said, 'You're unusually quiet this evening.'

'It's been a long day. I'm tired,' she riposted defensively.

'Of course…I'm sorry,' he said at once. 'I should have thought. I'll buy you a pick-me-up shortly.' He smiled in the darkness. 'I'd be very disappointed not to have the privilege of hearing your opinions this evening.'

Cryssie shuddered, but kept her cool. 'Oh, you'll get those,' she replied stiffly. There was a muffled sound beside her, which she correctly interpreted as suppressed amusement.

Neither of them spoke again for a few moments, and Jed contemplated the hours ahead. He could be in the company of any number of beautiful women—yet he'd felt impelled to ask this creature to spend New Year's Eve with him! His eyes narrowed momentarily. He hoped the evening would be worth it… Maybe, *maybe,* it might prove even more useful than he'd thought at first.

'Have you ever eaten at the Laurels before?' he asked, breaking the silence peremptorily, and making her start visibly.

'No,' she answered truthfully. 'Hydebound don't pay those

sort of wages—or at least they didn't,' she added mischievously, and she saw the corner of his mouth tilt crookedly in the way she was beginning to recognize. But he said nothing, leaning forward to adjust something in front of him, the sudden movement causing a drift of his aftershave to tease her nostrils.

'Well, I'm sure you won't be disappointed,' he said smoothly. 'And by the end of this evening I hope we will both feel that we understand each other a little more, and that our time has not been wasted.'

The restaurant was an imposing-looking Georgian building in the local countryside, and they were met by the manager, who greeted Jed effusively as he took Cryssie's jacket from her.

'Good evening, Mr Hunter,' he beamed, glancing covertly at Cryssie, taking in her appearance with one swift and critical glance. This was an unusual woman for one of the most dashing and important men on the planet to be escorting! Tonight of all nights! 'Your usual table is ready for you,' the man added purringly.

Cryssie, intensely sensitive to any new surroundings, was immediately aware of the manager's reaction to her. She knew she couldn't possibly compare favourably with Jeremy Hunter's women friends, but she'd already made up her mind that she was not going to let any feelings of inferiority bother her tonight. She was here for a formal reason, and it didn't matter that any second glances they attracted were directed at the man sitting opposite her rather than at her. For he looked outstandingly handsome, she had to admit, the elegance of his dinner suit complementing his physique, his strong features, his glossy black hair. He must have women fawning around him all the time—though if he expected that from her he was going to be disappointed!

Champagne arrived as if by magic, and the waiter filled Cryssie's glass to the brim, before pouring half a glass for Jed.

'Thanks, Simon,' Jed said easily, and the man moved away. He raised his flute, and looked at Cryssie, his sensuous eyes glittering in the candlelight. 'Let's drink to Hydebound,' he said coolly, 'and to a prosperous future for all of us.'

Cryssie raised her own glass and took two or three large gulps of the pale liquid, enjoying the feel of the bubbles in her mouth and throat, hardly able to believe that it was only a week ago that they'd been sitting together at another table—though not in quite so imposing surroundings!

She felt the expensive alcohol hit her stomach almost immediately, but it had the effect of relaxing her, and she put her glass down and looked around admiringly at the white-clothed tables, the discreet lighting, the valuable paintings on the walls, the luxurious drapes at the long windows.

'Who were you *really* going to bring here tonight?' she asked, feeling her guard slipping and not caring. Well, it was *obvious!* He'd been stood up—though she couldn't imagine who would *dare*—and had decided on the spur of the moment to make use of the table he'd booked, and grill her about his new staff.

He answered without hesitation. 'I hadn't intended bringing anyone,' he said, his lip curling dismissively. 'I have a table more or less permanently booked here—because I have a financial stake in the place. One of the perks of investing wisely,' he added, not at all perturbed at her very personal question.

'Oh,' Cryssie said, rather childishly, hastily drinking some more of the wine. So Jed Hunter owned—or part-owned—this as well. He was Mr Big, all right!

He'd hardly touched his drink, while her own glass was almost empty. He leaned across and refilled it for her, before taking up his large leather-bound menu and studying it for a few moments.

'I'm going to have the lobster, followed by pigeon,' he said matter-of-factly, as if he was describing sausage and mash!

Cryssie said faintly, 'Yes, that sounds…good. I'll have the same.'

The fact was, she'd never seen such a selection of food in her whole life, and it would have taken all the evening for her to make up her mind. But what was good enough for him was good enough for her!

He gave their order to the hovering waiter, and watched her silently while she sipped at her champagne. She'd stayed true to type, he mused, and had responded in exactly the way he would have expected. He had not fazed her in the slightest. She was still in total control of herself, yet there was that air of naïvety that made him feel protective of her! Heaven alone knew where she'd got that dress from—though the colour suited her well enough. Her hair was drawn primly back, as usual, shining with obvious health and fresh shampooing, and not a hint of make up had been applied to her face. Nor was a single item of jewellery anywhere to be seen. He took in all these details with a certain sense of satisfaction. It was as if she'd almost gone out of her way not to impress him, he thought. A most unusual and refreshing female—and a type he hadn't met before!

As the evening went on she proved to be an engaging conversationalist, answering his questions about Hydebound and its staff without any apparent evasiveness, and with extremely loyal and affectionate remarks about the previous owners. There was certainly no gossip or snippets of scandal which he might have been interested in. She was obviously a very worthy member of staff, he decided—someone who could prove useful to him in the future. His eyes narrowed briefly. He could spot a bargain a mile off.

'Why are you called Cryssie?' he asked suddenly, as they started helping themselves to the delicately presented food which had appeared. 'Is it Christine? Christina?'

Cryssie sighed as she looked down at her plate. 'I hate having to own up to my name,' she said resignedly. 'It's… Crystal.'

'So what's wrong with Crystal?' he asked mildly. 'I like it. It's…unusual.'

'Well, that's all right, then,' she replied tartly. 'But I *don't* like it. It's a silly name. How many people have you met called Crystal?'

'Not many. Not *any*. But I still like it.'

'Well, I'm not called Crystal. I'm called Cryssie.'

'Okay, Cryssie. I'll try to remember.'

She looked across at him, at his teasing, dangerous eyes. 'I shall have it changed properly one day,' she said, stabbing a spear of asparagus with her fork. 'I *will*.'

'I'm quite sure you will…Cryssie,' he said. 'I can't think that many of your plans come unstuck.' He paused. 'Do you have a grand life plan? I mean, you won't be wanting to stay with Hydebound for ever, I suppose?'

His question took Cryssie by surprise, and she shot him an anxious glance. The last thing she wanted was to be chucked out—or given the option to leave. She'd better watch what she was saying. Was this a veiled reference that he might not *want* her to stay? She shuddered briefly, trying to mix the unexpected—undeniable—pleasure of this evening with the upsetting news of the day.

'You said you're not married?' he persisted.

Before he could say anything more, she blurted out, 'No,

I'm not married, and I don't ever intend to be! I have Milo to consider, as well as my sister, who is ill most of the time. They both depend on me, and on what I earn. And I'm paid enough—and happy—at Hydebound. So I don't intend any immediate changes unless they're intended *for* me,' she added significantly, her heart missing a beat at hearing herself say those words. 'As for a "life plan", as you call it—well, the only one is for Milo, and his happiness.'

He regarded her coolly for a moment. 'Milo is lucky to have such a loving auntie,' he said quietly, catching her on the wrong foot. Well, he was good at that!

Cryssie looked away, biting her lip. 'I…I didn't say that Milo wasn't my son,' she said.

'No, you didn't. But I was studying the staff files this afternoon,' he said casually, 'and I saw that you live with your sister and her son. That's why I felt able to drag you away from the family nest on New Year's Eve.' He paused. 'Why? Is it a secret?'

'No, of course not,' Cryssie said hurriedly, realising that of course he would naturally have been checking all the files. Could find out whatever he wanted. 'The fact is…I actually look on Milo as my own son, and he's as *good* as my own son, because I shall never have any of my own and I don't want any. Not while I've got him. He loves me and I adore him, while Polly—my sister—really only lives for herself. And it's not her fault, because she's been ill since Milo was born and I don't think it's going to get any better. If anything should…happen…to her, I'd adopt Milo at once. So, since you ask, *that's* my life plan,' she added.

Her own words suddenly made hot tears spring to Cryssie's eyes. Of course she would love to have children of her own one day, who would grow up alongside her little nephew. But the bitterness of her past had tainted such plans for ever, had killed any trust in the honey-tongued male sex. She had believed every false word whispered to her during her six-month affair with the head of department in her very first job—a job she'd walked away from as soon as she'd realised the mess her life was becoming. And when she'd been offered employment by the elderly, kindly Lewis brothers she'd made another unconscious decision as well. That never again would she fall for the charms of a predatory and handsome employer who would use her not only in a business sense but in every other personal and emotional way too.

Jed observed her closely as she spoke, noting her misting eyes and the brief tremble of her lower lip. This woman was obviously intelligent, thoughtful… But there was an elusiveness about her which he found curiously heart-warming. She was clearly able to take care of herself, yet there was a simplicity about her that he found rather charming…and surprisingly sensually stimulating. Well, it was New Year's Eve—which might explain the sudden stirring in his loins!

'Your life plan sounds a very open-and-shut case for a young woman of your age,' he remarked casually. 'What do you have against the marriage contract?'

'Nothing,' Cryssie replied shortly. 'Just the long and winding road to reach that point. Never worth the trouble. Better to avoid it altogether.'

'So… You're happy to make do with second best?'

'What do you mean by that?' Cryssie said quickly.

'Merely that all your maternal instincts seem directed towards someone else's child. Bit of a waste, really. And no child needs two mothers.'

'You can look at it whichever way you like,' Cryssie said tightly. 'I'm completely happy with the decisions I've made.'

He picked up his glass and looked at the barely drunk champagne. He'd heard about *her* life plan—but as for his own? Well, they certainly had one big thing in common, he and his dinner companion. No wedding bells! At least not until his pride had recovered from the mega-bashing it had experienced. His main preoccupation was the continuation of the family empire. He'd managed to convince his parents that he could actually be trusted to take up the reins, allowing them more time for themselves at last, and he was enjoying the challenges of each day, plus the undoubted satisfaction of being in almost total control of a successful and respected business where his word was law.

CHAPTER THREE

IT WAS almost midnight, and the atmosphere in the crowded restaurant was heady and expectant. After the meal was over, a young up-and-coming group had entertained the gathering with popular numbers, and one or two couples had attempted to dance in the rather restricted space. During a lull, Cryssie had noticed that the manager had come up to Jed and murmured something in his ear, then moved away to speak to one or two other couples.

It was so warm and comfortable sitting here, Cryssie thought contentedly. Wining and dining had a lot going for it! She could get used to this sort of life! She watched the manager moving between the tables, and saw people glancing at their watches. Of course—the traditional countdown would soon begin. She supposed they'd all have to hold hands and sing 'Auld Lang Syne'! How embarrassing would that be? A horrible thought suddenly struck her, and she glanced at Jed, who must have been watching her, because their eyes met almost immediately. She swallowed, offering him a faint smile. What if everyone started kissing each other as they watched the widescreen television, switched on in one corner of the room, and listened to Big Ben strike at midnight? Wasn't it sort of *expected* on this occasion? Oh, no, please not that! she thought wildly. She would crawl under the table and die if she had to come into that close contact with her boss! But how could she act Miss Prim and Proper? It would look out of place, and very humiliating for Jed, if she cold-shouldered him and stood there like a lemon while everyone else in the room was slobbering over each other! This was one of those moments she was definitely not up to!

But she needn't have worried—Mr Know-it-all was equal to the situation, and when midnight finally arrived, and everyone jumped to their feet and cheered, and started singing the ancient song, Jed was immediately by her side, raising his glass in a toast.

'Happy New Year, Cryssie,' he said, above the noise. 'Let it be a good one for all of us.'

And that was it. The moment had passed, and she hadn't had to do anything! Jed was back in his place, smiling darkly across at her with that infuriatingly superior expression on his face which spoke volumes—and which implied that he knew exactly what *she'd* been thinking!

Why had she allowed herself to get in such a sweat? she thought crossly. Anyone would think she was eighteen again! Her hand trembled slightly as she sipped her drink. Would it have been so awful to perhaps feel Jed's warm hands at the nape of her neck, pulling her towards him? To feel his lips touch hers, if only for a moment? Or to sense his heart beating against her chest for a fraction of a second? She checked her thoughts abruptly. What on earth was the matter with her— was she *drunk?* Yes, that must be it! These sort of imaginings were not part of the deal between her and Jeremy Hunter. So why, then, was she feeling so…let down, so left out, so…*undesired?* Go on, admit it, she told herself fiercely. Why was she feeling so damned *disappointed?*

* * *

It was getting on for 1:00 a.m. when the manager used the loud speaker system to address the still almost full gathering; only a few couples having already left.

'Ladies and gents…guys…' he began, as someone raised a drunken cheer. 'I have been passing the word around, but as it's nearly time to call it a day I should warn you that it's not getting any better outside, and some of you are going to have difficulty getting home tonight.'

Mild consternation greeted his words, and people began to stand up. Cryssie frowned as she looked across at Jed.

'What's going on? What is it?' she asked.

'Oh—just that it's been snowing on and off for most of the evening, that's all,' he said casually. 'But as there's nothing anyone can do about that I wasn't going to spoil the occasion by bothering you with the information.'

Snow! That was news to her! But she realised she hadn't heard any weather forecasts over the last day or so. 'What did he mean that we'd have difficulty getting home?' she asked childishly. 'Your car is well equipped to deal with changes in the weather, isn't it?'

She wished that she didn't feel so unlike herself as she spoke…so strange… But then, was that a surprise? She'd never drunk champagne before in her life, and her usual wisdom and common sense seemed to have deserted her in allowing Jed to refill her glass all the evening. Neither had she ever spent this most poignant night of the year with such a handsome member of the opposite sex! It was certainly the funniest business meeting *she'd* ever attended!

She tried to get to her feet, then sat down again hurriedly.

He picked up a large jug of water and poured some into a glass. 'Here—dilute the alcohol a bit,' he ordered. 'I'll go outside and take a look.' He held her anxious gaze for a second, a rush of something he couldn't explain sweeping over him. 'Don't worry—*Crystal*,' he said evenly, and his use of her name made her glower. 'It'll be okay.'

It had *better* be okay, she thought, as she sipped at the water. But of course it would… Even the weather wouldn't dare interfere with Mr Jeremy Hunter's plans! He'll get it sorted, she reassured herself. And anyway, the Laurels wasn't *that* far away from home…only about five or six miles, if she'd judged the distance right. Home! Why wasn't she there now, safely tucked up in bed?

There was a general hubbub in the room as everyone made plans to leave, and presently Jed returned to the table, an unusually rueful expression on his face.

'You've been ages,' Cryssie said, looking up at him. 'What have you been doing—building a snowman?'

'No, nor taking part in any snowball fights either,' he replied pleasantly. 'I've been checking with the police about the prospect of our journey home. This blizzard—or rather, the intensity of it—was totally unexpected. A few showers were anticipated, that's all, with more to follow mid-week. But nothing like this. And it's still coming down—you can hardly see your hand in front of your face. Several of the higher roads are already impassable, and the ploughs won't be out until the morning—if then.' He ran a hand through his hair, which was wet and speckled with glistening white flakes. The unusually dishevelled look gave him an alluringly boyish appearance, Cryssie thought briefly.

She stood up, still uncertain on her feet, and he automatically cupped his hand under her elbow.

'I should sit there for a bit,' he advised. 'There's no rush.'

'What do you mean there's no rush?' she demanded, her voice sounding shriller than she'd meant it to. 'Oughtn't we to be setting off? Everyone else seems to be going,' she added, glancing around at the now practically empty room.

'Quite a few of the guests live fairly close by, apparently, and will have no problem walking home. Some might even make it in their cars, with a bit of luck—if they haven't got that far to go. But I'm afraid those of us living in town haven't a hope in hell.'

'Well, we shall all just have to start walking back together, then,' Cryssie said firmly. 'There's safety in numbers, and it shouldn't take that long, should it?' She stood up, suddenly feeling alert and decisive.

'No, Cryssie,' Jed said patiently. 'I thought you were a bright girl. Just think of the dress you're wearing, the jacket you came in, and your…um…sandals.' He glanced down at her feet, and Cryssie winced as he itemised her rather pathetic outfit. 'How far do you think you'd get in those?'

'I take your point,' she said stoutly. 'But I'll be fine—honestly,' she added. 'If we walk briskly I'll keep warm enough, and wet feet aren't the most life-threatening things in the world, are they? I'll survive.'

Her words sounded bright enough, but she had to admit to a sinking feeling as she spoke. It would not be easy, she realised that, trudging through snowdrifts, but what other option was there? It didn't even occur to her to consider his own mode of dress—as equally unsuitable as hers for this sort of situation. The only thing on her mind was that they should depart from this place, and the sooner the better!

He put his hands on her shoulders and looked down into her upturned face, into her green eyes which were bright and alive, like those of a small animal facing a predator. 'Cryssie—I'm sorry—but there is no way we can get home tonight. It would be madness to attempt driving—we'd probably get stuck, unable to move forward or back. And walking is *not* an option—for either of us. It's much too far. We shall just have to sit this out until the morning, when it's light and we can see more clearly what's ahead of us.' He dropped his hands to his sides and shrugged. 'I'm sorry. I— no one—had any idea that this would happen. It's just one of those things.'

Cryssie stared at him blankly for a moment, her brain suddenly refusing to function. 'So what are we going to do, then? Stay *here* all night?' she demanded. 'We can't do that— I *must* get home. They'll wonder what's happened—Polly will be frantic!' Well, when she eventually wakes up, Cryssie thought briefly. Her sister was not an early riser, and hadn't managed to get Milo his breakfast for years.

'Well, I'm sure your sister will put two and two together,' Jed said dryly. 'Ring her now, leave a message on the answer-machine, or send her a text explaining the situation so that she knows when she wakes up. Really, Cryssie, don't look so…dramatic,' he added, noting her desperate expression. 'This is not the beginning of the end of the world.'

Cryssie plonked herself down on her chair. How on earth was she going to sit here all night making small talk with Jed Hunter? She was suddenly dead tired, and, sighing deeply, she raised her eyes to his.

'Well, it's a good thing it's Bank Holiday tomorrow—or should I say today?' she said. 'Because I'm fit for nothing if I don't get my sleep. I'm afraid you wouldn't have your money's worth out of me if we had to go to work in the morning.'

'Oh, I'll make sure you get your sleep,' he assured her. 'Even if it is to be a short night.'

'And how exactly are you going to do *that?*' she retorted,

feeling alarmed and distinctly rattled at the way things were turning out. 'I can't sleep sitting up…'

'You won't have to,' he said briefly. 'They're letting me have one of their rooms.'

'Uh? What do you mean?' she asked stupidly. 'This is not a hotel—it's a restaurant.'

'It's a hotel-restaurant—with a few rooms. Four, to be exact,' Jed explained patiently. 'And we, and a few others, have been lucky enough to be allotted one. The less fortunate will be making themselves comfortable wherever they can.'

Naturally! Cryssie thought at once. He'd said he had a financial interest in the place, so they'd make sure Jed Hunter's needs were taken care of!

Just then, the manager came up to them. 'Everything's ready for you, Mr Hunter,' the man said. 'Room one—at the top of the staircase.' He smiled down at Cryssie. 'These are not the usual circumstances under which we welcome our guests,' he said cheerfully, 'but it's a very comfortable room— the best one, actually,' he added. 'You'll find everything you need there.'

'Thanks, Mark,' Jed said, taking Cryssie's arm firmly and pulling her to her feet. 'We'll be fine. Thank you for accommodating us.'

Cryssie stared up at him, open-mouthed and incredulous. 'Now, hang on a minute—' she began, but he cut in.

'Come on…darling,' he said lightly, and there was a warning note in the word. 'It's way past your bedtime. Goodnight, Mark—and thanks again,' he added, to the man's retreating back.

Come on *what? Who?* I'm not his darling, she thought wildly, anger beginning to take over. Did he *really* think she was going to spend the night alone with him—as if it was the most natural thing in the world? Well, it might be natural for *him* to share his bed with the female companion of the moment, but *her* life was not like that! And it never would be!

'Now, you look *here*—' she began, trotting briskly along the carpeted hallway in an attempt to keep up with his determined stride, trying to free her arm from his strong grasp. 'If you think for a single minute that I—'

'Don't make a scene, Cryssie,' he said roughly. 'I'm known in this place.'

So, whatever else happened, Mr Jeremy Hunter mustn't lose face! If she 'made a scene', as he put it, and refused to go along with his plans, it would make him look so small, so uncool! So humiliated! That any woman wouldn't *want* to be whisked off to bed with him was unthinkable! After all, this was the twenty-first century. Who demanded single rooms in this day and age? She doubted whether there was a female in the world who wouldn't jump at the chance to be in her position!

She felt completely and utterly helpless as he marched her up the stairs, and inserted the key to their room, opening the door and pushing her inside in front of him.

'Mmm,' he said appreciatively. 'This looks cosy enough, don't you think?' He glanced across at the large double bed, then looked down at her quizzically. 'Which side do you prefer?'

He was laughing at her now—teasing her—that was obvious. His black eyes were dancing with merriment, and that just served to make her give him a piece of her mind.

'If you think—for one *second*—that I'm going to spend the night here, with you…I mean…it's unthinkable!' she began.

He raised one dark eyebrow. 'So? What are you going to do? Spend it outside on the landing? That would be most uncomfortable, not to say ungrateful, and bewildering to the management. They'll think this room isn't good enough for madam.'

She looked at him witheringly, but before she could speak again he said more tersely, 'Don't be a foolish girl, Cryssie. You're tired and you need some rest, and this is obviously the best—the only—way out of this.' He looked down at her steadily. 'Don't get so uptight. It'll all look different in the morning.'

'Let's hope you're right,' she said flatly. 'You might think that this is all part of a jolly evening, *Jeremy*,' she said furiously, then stopped short as she heard herself utter his name. Because it was the first time she had called him anything at all.

'Please—do call me Jed,' he said amiably, as he began to loosen his bow tie. 'All my friends do. And after tonight I think we really will be like...old friends—don't you?'

She hoped she wasn't reading more into that than he meant! But if he *did* have any big ideas he was going to be disappointed! She realised that this incredible evening had proved one thing—she didn't care if she had a job next week or not. It no longer seemed that important. And if it meant she'd be told to find something else—well, it was just too bad. She would not be manipulated by this man. He seemed able to manipulate everyone else, but she wouldn't let him get away with it this time!

'Let's get one thing straight,' she said tartly. 'I am not your darling, thank you very much, and I take exception to your use of the word.'

'Okay,' he said evenly. 'I only called you that to save us both unnecessary embarrassment. It would have looked far worse to give the impression that we were comparative strangers about to share a room than to make it look as if we were—well, happily acquainted, shall we say?'

Cryssie had to admit that he had a point. Suddenly her shoulders drooped, and for an awful moment she thought she was going to burst into tears. But she wasn't going to give him the satisfaction of seeing her crumble. She wasn't finished yet! Instead, she marched over to the two-seater settee under the window and threw her bag down on to it.

'It will give me great pleasure to allow you to have the use of the bed yourself, *Jed*,' she said defiantly, 'because I won't be sleeping on either side.' She glanced down. 'This will suit me just great, as long as I can have a blanket and a pillow.' She glared up at him. 'I'll be fine,' she added, realising that although in one way she felt absolutely shattered, she was now wide awake and in charge of her emotions, and it filled her with a sense of superiority.

He shook his head gently from side to side as she spoke, as he might at a difficult child. 'We could put something down the middle of the bed, you know—to keep us well apart...' he began, then stopped as she turned to give him another mouthful. 'Okay, okay, Cryssie—anything you say,' he said quickly. He took off his jacket and draped it over the back of a chair, and Cryssie swallowed. Was the man going to start undressing in front of her? she thought. 'Why don't you use the facilities first?' he added, in a conciliatory tone. 'Take your time. Don't mind me.'

Thankful for the chance to escape before he took off anything else, Cryssie went immediately into the adjoining bathroom and shut and locked the door. Sitting on the edge of the bath for a moment, with her head in her hands, she wondered how on earth she'd landed in this predicament. The stuff of silly dreams! Whatever would Polly say if she ever dared tell her—or anyone else, for that matter—how, where and with whom she'd been forced to spend the night?

Standing up slowly, she looked around her. Hung up against the door were two white towelling robes—great! She would sleep very comfortably in one of those, she thought.

She slipped out of her dress and underwear, thinking that it was a bit late to have a bath, but a warm shower suddenly seemed irresistible. She switched it on, grateful for all the complementary toiletries there on the shelf, and she soaped and shampooed luxuriously, suddenly feeling up-beat for a brief second or two. After all, she'd never stayed in a place like this, nor spent a night in any hotel in her life. This was luxury, and she should try and enjoy it, she told herself.

Then she thought of what—or who—was on the other side of the door, and her mood plummeted again instantly. She'd better hurry and take up her position on that sofa—and pray that morning and a rapid thaw would come quickly! And that this whole episode could be over with and forgotten—if that were possible!

Using one of the several huge white fluffy towels, she dried herself, and her hair, as best she could…there didn't seem to be a hairdryer—completing the exercise with the liberal use of the powder and fragrances so thoughtfully supplied. Then, taking a deep breath, she opened the door softly, peeping out, hoping that Jed would be already fast asleep, and that no more words need be said that night.

No such luck. As she emerged he was there, totally undressed apart from a pair of boxers, stretched out casually on the bed, with his hands clasped behind his head. Cryssie caught her breath, for even with the quickest of glances that she'd shot him she was breathtakingly aware of the mat of dark hair under his armpits and across his sun-tanned chest, of his long legs and taut, muscular thighs, all encompassing a finely toned and athletic, vigorous body.

She averted her eyes quickly, before there was time to admire anything else! And he watched her as she padded across the room in her bare feet. He smiled inwardly. She was certainly nature unadorned, he thought, with her long, damp hair curling around her shoulders, her body completely concealed amongst the folds of the over-sized robe. Yet, oddly, the healthily natural picture she presented was as acutely desirable as any of the women he'd ever met.

He swung his legs over the side of the bed and made for the bathroom. 'You smell wonderful,' he said, glancing across at her.

'Thanks to the management,' Cryssie said coolly. 'I've left plenty for you.'

He turned as if to say something, then thought better of it and went into the bathroom. Cryssie noted with a stab of appreciation that he'd made her up a bed on the sofa. He had taken the duvet and made a sort of nest, complete with two pillows, leaving himself just one, plus a cover. She hoped he'd be warm enough—then she shrugged. Jed Hunter was well able to take care of himself—and so was she! She snuggled down, thinking that ever since she and Mr Jeremy Hunter had met her life seemed to have been running away with her! And she was having difficulty keeping up!

It was surprisingly comfortable on the sofa, she thought— though it was a good thing she wasn't any taller, since her toes just reached the bottom edge. All in all, things could be worse, she thought sleepily, and whatever she thought of the man, one thing was certain—he was not likely to ravish her, to overpower her. Enveloped in her cosy cocoon, she smiled to herself. *What* a shame for poor Jeremy Hunter that he'd picked the wrong woman to help him celebrate the start of the new year! Because he could get lost if he'd ever thought of her as a one-night stand!

In the bathroom, Jed dried himself briskly, drawing the huge towel back and forth across his broad shoulders, his glistening muscles flexing and hardening with the effort.

Leaning forward, he rubbed at the mirror on the wall with his fist, to allow his reflection to appear through the misty glass. He paused for a second, and the hint of a smile crossed his elegant features. The evening was obviously not to have the passionate conclusion he might have wished for under other circumstances... Not that *that* had been his intention tonight. Far from it! Yet it was funny how things might work out, he thought. Profit and loss were no strangers to *him*. They were part of the balance sheet of life. It was the final account that was important.

Reaching for the remaining robe on the back of the door, he shrugged himself into it and paused, his eyes narrowing for a second. His first instincts about the woman had been pretty sound, he thought—as all his instincts usually were. She could prove to be very, very useful to him in the future— if he could get her on his side. It was obvious there was going to be strong opposition to his plans in some quarters, but he'd get his own way in the end. As long as he didn't throw the baby out with the bathwater! He smiled darkly to himself. He knew how to please women, knew their sensitive points, both physical and emotional. But this particular woman was different. He'd known that from the moment he'd set eyes on her. When he'd arrived so unexpectedly at the office that morning she'd seemed totally indifferent, although he was sure she must remember their conversation in his own shop, and the remarks she'd made—not all of them complimentary!

Silently, he went into the bedroom and stared down at the inert figure on the sofa. She was fast asleep, breathing deeply, dead to the world. He paused, his fertile mind in overdrive, as usual. Then, bending, he picked her up effortlessly in his arms and carried her across to the bed.

CHAPTER FOUR

A COLD white light filtering in through a crack in the curtains met Cryssie's sleepy gaze as she struggled to rouse herself from deep slumber. For several seconds she lay there, totally unable to get a grip on herself. This wasn't her own bed...this was a large, deliciously comfortable double bed, the luxurious duvet wrapping itself around her extravagantly. Stretching, she curled her toes in warm and blissful comfort, before suddenly memory—and her true situation—hit her like something hurtling from outer space.

Easing herself into a half-sitting position, she rested on one elbow and looked around her cautiously. There was no sign of Jed, or any of his clothes, and on the sofa lay the one pillow and the cover, which had been neatly folded.

Aware that her heart had gone into racing mode, Cryssie flopped back and stared up at the ceiling. What had gone on last night? And why was she here, and not on that sofa? Swallowing nervously, she loosened the belt of her bathrobe and smoothed her hand over the flat plane of her stomach, testing her muscles and reflexes for a sign—any sign—that anything of an intimate nature might have taken place. Though it beggared belief that she wouldn't have known about it!

She knew immediately that absolutely nothing had

happened to her while she'd slept—the fleeting thought of that possibility discounted in a split second. She knew that Jed Hunter would not have taken advantage of her in that way, and anyway… He would have expected a co-operative lover who would enjoy and participate in his physical attentions, not an unconscious and passive partner!

She paused, letting her thoughts run on for a few moments. But she had not *walked* across to this bed—he must have carried her here. The realisation that she'd been so exhausted and out of it as not to have been aware of that, was deeply disturbing. Quite simply she'd been totally at his mercy, and her vulnerability came as delayed shock, so that her heart raced again and she trembled slightly, sitting up now, and running her hand through her tousled hair. Her mouth felt dry and unpleasant from the alcohol she'd drunk last night, and what she really longed for most was a large mug of hot tea.

As if in answer to her thoughts, the door opened and Jed came in, carrying a tray holding a glass of orange juice, a small pot of tea and a rack of warm toast. In spite of everything Cryssie couldn't help smiling as he came across to the side of the bed and, glancing down at her, said smoothly, 'Ah—glad to see you've surfaced at last.'

He placed the tray on the bedside table and looked down at her in a way that made her heart beat even faster! He certainly had the advantage over her—again—because he had obviously shaved and showered, and looked fantastic—as always.

Seeing her amused expression, he raised one eyebrow in that maddeningly special way that made Cryssie's toes curl. 'What's funny?' he enquired mildly.

'You,' Cryssie said, trying not to giggle. 'You look like the head waiter!'—for obviously he was in his evening dress. 'Thank you, my good man. I hope you don't expect a tip!'

The minute she'd said that she regretted it, because it gave him the perfect opportunity to say that he did—and what *sort* of tip! But he merely grinned at her and walked across to the window, drawing the curtains aside.

'What time is it?' she asked, in a still sleepy voice, reaching for the glass of orange juice and drinking thirstily.

'Ten-thirty,' he replied. 'With a bit of luck I can get you home by late afternoon. The thaw has arrived as suddenly as the storm, but slush is now the problem, so it'll take a while. But the ploughs have been busy since daylight.' He turned to look across at her. 'Do you feel better this morning? You've had a very restful night, considering everything.'

'Yes, thanks,' Cryssie said, pouring herself some tea. 'And thank you for letting me have the bed…. Did you manage to get any rest on that thing?'

'Not a lot,' he admitted, 'but that doesn't matter. I can go without sleep for hours. As you'd informed me earlier that you need yours, it was only sensible for us to swap.' He paused, noting the pretty blush which coloured her cheeks as she sipped the warm tea. Why did he *feel* this way, so *protective* of this unprepossessing female? he asked himself. 'I must say, you look very…refreshed this morning.'

She looked at him thoughtfully for a moment, marvelling privately at how fate had managed to bring her to this position in her usually uneventful existence. 'Have you had break-fast?' she asked suddenly. And what did it matter to her whether he had or not? she thought fleetingly. Yet somehow it did… He had been—was being—very considerate. A pang of something she couldn't explain seared her heart for a moment. Under other circumstances, and happening to someone other than herself, this would be a wonderful situa-tion, she thought. To be sitting up in bed being brought breakfast by a handsome member of the opposite sex would surely be the stuff of romance. Romance! That dangerous word was nothing to do with her!

'I've had coffee,' he replied, turning to look out of the window again. 'We might have some lunch here later, if you feel like it, and then try the roads.' He paused, and then without looking at her went on quietly, 'There's no need for anyone at Hydebound to know what happened, by the way…that we couldn't get home last night,' he said. 'Or indeed that we were here at all. I never discuss my private life and arrangements with anyone anyway—certainly no one in business—and I'd advise you to do likewise. It saves a lot of gossip and chit-chat. If by some chance word gets around, all anyone needs to know is that I needed to talk to you about work—which I did—and that we were holed up here because of the snow but spent the night apart—which we also did.' He turned and looked across at her. 'The management here are discretion itself, so nothing will come from this direction. It is, after all, our business. And it should remain that way.'

Cryssie had started to butter a piece of toast while he'd been speaking, but now his words made her put down her knife and push the plate aside, any appetite completely gone. 'I will say nothing to anyone,' she said coldly. 'I left a message for my sister last night, so she knows why I couldn't get home. But other than that my lips are sealed!'

He needn't worry himself about his mighty reputation being damaged in any way by *her*, she thought angrily. Last night had been *his* idea, not hers, and if he wanted it all kept secret that was fine by her! In any case, she would not have dreamed of mentioning it at work. Rose could be spiteful at times, and it wouldn't be wise for *her* to know anything!

Jed smiled at her darkly, but somehow Cryssie couldn't

even begin to smile back. She was honest enough to realise that she had warmed to Jeremy Hunter—a no doubt essential person in their lives, hers and Polly's and Milo's—had even begun to like him. A lot. But his calculating statement just now had wiped that from her mind. He was only interested in himself and his standing in the community, she thought.

She drank the last of her tea and threw off the duvet. 'I'd better get dressed,' she said coolly. 'Because the minute the roads are open I want to get home.'

'Of course—we both do,' he replied. 'As for tomorrow I'll be interviewing all the staff individually, so perhaps you'd see that all the personal files are available?'

'That's the secretary's responsibility,' Cryssie said. 'Rose Jacobs. She's perfectly capable of carrying out your every wish.' She walked across to the bathroom and glanced back at him over her shoulder. 'Thank you for dinner last night,' she said. 'I had never tasted anything like that before, and it was…special.'

He stared across at her, his black eyes boring into her gentle green ones. She needn't have confessed to her ignorance of the finer things in life, he thought. Could have pretended that dining in a place like the Laurels was not a new experience. Her simplicity of nature touched him again. No other woman he'd ever been with had had this effect on him. She was undemanding and unpretentious, yet no shrinking violet either, and some of her comments last night had made him laugh out loud. His usual women-friends weren't generally known for their sense of humour…

By mid afternoon they were on their way back to town, and when he drew up outside her front gate he turned briefly to look at her, wondering what was going through her head. She had been very quiet today, he thought, all the easy familiarity of last night completely gone, her quick-witted remarks non-existent.

'Are you okay, Cryssie?' he asked casually.

'I'm perfectly okay, thank you—Jeremy,' she replied. 'And don't worry—I'll remember to call you Mr. Hunter from now on.'

A sudden look of realisation crossed his features for a second, and he gripped her wrist roughly. 'If you're referring to my suggestion that we should be discreet about last night,' he said curtly, 'I can assure you that it was for your sake, not mine!'

'Of course it was, Jeremy,' she said sweetly.

And with that she opened her door and got out before he could help her, or say another word.

The following day it was business as usual, and as soon as Cryssie got to work she saw that Jed had already arrived. Parking her car a long way away from the silver Porsche, she ran up the stairs to the office, where Rose was booting up the computers.

'Hi, Rose,' she said breathlessly, taking off her coat. 'Did you have a good New Year's Eve?'

'Oh—so-so,' the woman replied. 'You?'

'Oh…yes, as usual,' Cryssie replied vaguely, crossing her fingers as she did so. She couldn't describe *her* New Year's Eve as so-so! 'Have you seen Mr Hunter yet? His car's here.'

'Yes,' Rose replied. 'He put his head around the door a few minutes ago. Wants to see us all one by one. He's instructed me to bring him the relevant files,' she added importantly. .

As they got on with their work, Rose said, 'What do you think of our new boss, then, Cryssie? Do you think our jobs really are safe—for the time being at least? Or will he start making changes that'll force us to resign? Or maybe we'll be chucked out!'

Cryssie kept her eyes on her computer. 'Why ask me, Rose?'

'Oh…only that you have met him before, haven't you? I just thought you might have some inside knowledge, that's all.'

'Our acquaintance was just a passing encounter in Latimer's,' Cryssie said. 'I was a customer—and I sort of complained about something—and he just happened to be around at the time.'

'Well, you have to agree that he's a looker,' Rose said, sighing briefly. 'I don't think any of us would throw him out of bed, do you?'

'Probably not,' Cryssie replied, turning her face away, aware that it was burning.

'I wonder whether sir likes coffee at eleven o'clock,' Rose said as she took another batch of files from the cabinet. 'And whether he likes milk, and one lump or two?'

'Oh, he—' Cryssie almost said that he liked it black with no sugar, but stopped herself just in time! 'Just put everything on the tray and let him help himself,' she said quickly.

Presently Rose left the room with the things that Jed wanted, and Cryssie sat back for a moment. She hadn't dropped any bricks so far, she thought, but it was hard to try and eradicate her recent experiences from her mind. To say the whole business was unreal, not to say surreal, was an understatement! And the mental picture of her employer lying on the bed, naked apart from his boxers, still made her senses rush. She admitted to herself for the first time, and reluctantly, how close she might have come to lying beside him, to allowing those long, sensitive fingers to caress her body. And now she was expected to forget everything and pretend it had never happened. It was simply an impossibility. Nothing about Jeremy Hunter was unforgettable!

Swallowing hard, she reached for the bottle of water she

kept by her side and sipped. She must keep reminding herself
that so far as the man was concerned the evening had been in-
consequential, unimportant. It must be obvious to him that she
could never compete with all the women he had bedded in his
lifetime, and from a sexual point of view she had nothing that
would satisfy him. She knew that. And she cringed again as
she remembered his almost curt directive that their evening
and night together must remain a closely guarded secret. The
thought of her name being linked with his in any other way
than business would hardly add to his professional or personal
standing! *However* much he'd tried to excuse his directive!
Well, as she had assured him, her lips were sealed.

Almost at the end of the day, the internal buzzer sounded
and Cryssie was summoned to enter the office so recently
vacated by the Lewis brothers. She couldn't help feeling a
tinge of sadness to see their place taken by someone else—
even if it was by the rich and gorgeous Mr J. Hunter!

He stood up as she came in, indicating the chair at the
other side of the desk where he was sitting. In spite of herself
Cryssie felt her mouth dry up as she looked at him squarely.
Even someone like Rose—well on in years and happily
married—had made it clear that she would find a night alone
with the man appealing! And today, in this dusty office, he was
certainly that. He was well turned out, as always, but his dark
hair seemed to fall more carelessly over his forehead than
usual, and it made Cryssie want to put out her hand and
smooth it gently. Stop! she told herself. That night is history!
Any such familiar thoughts were out of order! And, as well as
that, these teenage feelings were not part of her agenda—they
had been buried long ago. But she realised with growing
concern that he was filling more of her thoughts than was good
for her—for either of them. She must keep her eye firmly fixed

on the goal ahead—which was to constantly improve her prospects so that she need never feel afraid for Milo and his future.

'Sit down, Cryssie,' he said formally, and their eyes locked for a second as he looked across at her. 'I take it that your family were not unduly alarmed at your delay in returning home from the Laurels?' he added quietly.

'They weren't alarmed at all, thank you,' Cryssie answered—which was true. Polly had barely expressed any interest in what the 'meeting' had been about, her only reaction being amusement in seeing Cryssie turning up still dressed in her long frock. But Milo had rushed into her arms and showered her with kisses, demanding that she must come and play with him.

Jed didn't even bother to open the file with her name on it, but leaned back and glanced up at her from beneath his dark eyebrows, his expression cool. Cryssie would have loved to be able to read his thoughts... Did they match her own? she wondered. The memory of their time together would be impinged for ever on *her* consciousness!

'I have very little to discuss with you,' he said casually. 'I think we know each other reasonably well, and you've told me most of what I need to know.' He paused. 'The Lewises have given you a very good recommendation, saying that your figures were always in order and everyone got paid on time.' Cryssie said nothing, so he continued. 'Also that you are very popular with the rest of the staff. Relationships are important,' he added, shooting her a quick glance.

'In a close-knit environment that's certainly true,' Cryssie ventured. 'But the staff are really happy here—happy with their lot.'

She hoped he was getting her message: that he shouldn't start making a clean sweep through the firm, upsetting everything and everybody.

'Our previous discussions have made my meeting now with you unnecessary,' he went on coolly, 'but I thought it might look strange not to ask you to come in as everyone else has done.'

But of course, Cryssie thought—don't let's forget our big secret!

He looked up then, and added, 'So that will be all, for the moment.'

Looking at her, as she sat with her hands clasped anxiously in her lap, suddenly made him want to say something to reassure her. But instead he got up abruptly, indicating that the meeting was over.

Cryssie waited for a second before throwing discretion to the winds. 'I…we…are all very anxious to know what your plans are, Mr Hunter. No one feels safe. Will we all have our jobs next year?' She swallowed. Why was she bothering to ask him? she thought. Wasn't he just the sort of employer she'd vowed never to work for ever again? But for the moment she couldn't afford to be choosy! She needed the money!

He moved across towards her and looked down into her upturned face. 'We do, naturally, have plans for the company,' he said smoothly, 'but at this stage it would be unwise to say anything.' He placed a hand briefly on her arm, feeling her tremble perceptibly. 'Hydebound must change course—must develop and move on. Every company must, or die. You should know that. Something has to happen here. The firm cannot linger on, getting more and more into debt.' He paused. 'But try not to worry too much. You will all be informed in plenty of time as to if and when you are likely to be affected.'

Cryssie shook her head forlornly. 'It's not a good season of the year to have this kind of upheaval,' she said, rather stupidly. 'I for one can do without it.'

'I'm sorry about that,' he said dryly. 'I can see that I must improve on my timing.'

And that was that. Cryssie went back to her office no wiser. It was possible that some of them would be retained—but what of the rest?

Cryssie found it hard to stop her eyes filling with tears. But was that surprising? She was tired and confused…but mostly confused…at the rollercoaster of her emotions.

Rose, who was packing up to go home, looked at her curiously. 'What's up with you?' she asked. 'He wasn't unpleasant, was he?' She picked up her bag. 'I found him very charming—though not particularly forthcoming. Meeting us all was a mere formality, wasn't it?'

'No, he wasn't unpleasant,' Cryssie said. 'But I feel sure something's afoot that's not going to suit everyone.'

'Why—what's he been saying?'

'Only that all companies must move on. I don't know what he actually meant by that, but I'm pretty certain that where he's concerned there's no sentiment in business.' She turned off her computer and turned to the older woman. 'Oh, Rose, I just wish that the Lewises were still here and that everything was back to normal! And I really, really, really wish that Jeremy Hunter didn't exist at all!' she added emphatically.

'Hark at you,' Rose said. 'Never mind—he'll probably keep *us* on. Especially if we keep on the right side of him. Men like him enjoy having submissive females around to massage their massive egos.'

'Well, as far as I'm concerned he'd better not hold his breath,' Cryssie said, switching off the light.

Meanwhile, as he stared moodily out of the window, his hands thrust in his pockets, Jed Hunter's mind was working overtime. The woman had made the point only too well that disruptions to her life were unwelcome—well, she'd better get used to it, he thought. But there was one important detail to be sorted first… He had to find out just what kind of female she really was. Was she as impervious to male attentions as she appeared? Or was her coolness, her deliberate coolness with him, an act? His eyes narrowed as his mind went back over the events at the Laurels. Then his lip curled ever so slightly. He'd find out—sooner rather than later!

CHAPTER FIVE

IF SHE'D thought that her life was going to resume some sort of normality, Cryssie was in for a shock. A few weeks later Jed called her into his office, barely looking up as she sat down.

He finished what he was writing, glancing at her covertly from beneath his dark eyebrows. He couldn't stop himself remembering the night that she'd lain in that big double bed, so fast asleep, with her lashes—surprisingly long, as he'd taken the time to notice—fluttering now and again as she breathed and dreamed. He was beginning to feel irritable with himself at the number of times she was creeping into his thoughts—and not always in a business sense either!

Now, he flipped his pen down on the desk. 'Cryssie, things are going to move faster than I thought,' he began. 'I wanted you to be the first to know about it.'

Cryssie swallowed, trying to stem the ripple of anxiety that ran through her. The tone he was using didn't sound as if the news was good. He came straight to the point.

'I…we…intend winding Hydebound up,' he said flatly. 'The building is to be demolished to make way for a big hotel.' He waited for her to say something, but when she just stared at him unbelievingly he went on quickly. 'I wanted you to know first,' he said again, 'before all the rumours and chit-chat begin—which they undoubtedly will, because the planning application has already gone in to the Council. I shall call a meeting tomorrow to tell the rest of the staff.'

'Do you mean that the firm…that Hydebound…will cease to exist…will die?' Cryssie's voice was no more than a horrified whisper, and in spite of himself Jed felt a pang of discomfort. Then he pulled himself together. This was business. He was a businessman!

'I realise this is not going to be pleasant for everyone,' he said calmly. 'But it can't be helped. We shall therefore not be accepting any more orders, but will naturally honour those already in hand.'

He paused, noting that her hands trembled slightly, and that a deep, rosy blush had begun to sweep over her features. But her green eyes were bright and candid, and she returned his gaze unflinchingly.

'I think that the orders should be finalised by March or April, and I envisage a complete shutdown by June. All the staff will be paid up to then, with final redundancy bonuses added at the end.' His tone was clipped and formal. 'In the meantime, everyone will be entitled to look around for other employment. And there will be some opportunities in the new place. I'll help where I can.'

He picked up his pen again and twirled it between his fingers.

'I'm relying on the co-operation and goodwill of the staff—yours, too, Cryssie. You're obviously a very popular member of the team, so perhaps you can help there. Pour oil on troubled waters.'

Huh! So he thought she'd try and make things easy for him, did he? Bail him out! Cryssie felt almost frozen to the spot, but she finally found her voice again. 'So. We're all finished, then. Redundant. And you're going to kill off a family firm that's traded happily for almost half a century.'

He nodded. 'That's about it,' he said, unperturbed. 'And I can assure you that the new enterprise will be very good for the town. Good for the local economy.'

For a long, timeless moment complete silence reigned.

'You unspeakable pig,' she said, her voice deadly quiet.

'I beg your pardon?' His tone was equally deadly, and there was no hint of warmth in those dangerously seductive eyes as he returned her gaze.

'What an absolutely vile, *horrible* thing to do! To wipe us off the face of the earth to satisfy your materialistic lust! Who says the town needs another hotel? There are two already!'

'Yes, and they're as out-of-date as Hydebound is,' he replied curtly. 'Visitors are always complaining that there's nowhere decent to stay. So I'll put that right. It'll be upmarket, with a swimming pool and other leisure facilities. In just the right place—here, on the outskirts of town, with plenty of space for car parking, countryside all around. It couldn't be better!'

'Oh, yes—for *you,* perhaps!' Cryssie almost shouted at him. 'But do you realise how many lives you're affecting— what this will *mean* to us?'

'Don't be so dramatic, Cryssie,' he said firmly. 'Those young enough and able enough will find other work—and, as I said, I'll do all I can to help. There will be hotel jobs going when the time comes—and that'll be sooner than you think.'

'But many of the staff here are *craftsmen*—not hotel workers! What sort of a deal would that be to *them?*'

'In today's world we must all be flexible,' he countered. 'And if they apply to Latimer's I'll see they're given every consideration. People can't expect to have a job for life, for heaven's sake!'

Cryssie was finding difficulty keeping herself under control. Any liking she might have had for the man had completely disappeared.

'People have mortgages to pay!' she flared, her eyes bright with indignation. 'How *dare* you take it upon yourself to decide whether they might or might not be able to keep roofs over their heads! They are *expert* at their jobs, and—'

'So why, then, has Hydebound been running at considerable loss for years?' He paused, and looked down at her for a second or two. 'No firm can sustain itself on good workmanship alone. Many other things have to be considered. Just look at the distance from town, for a start…there's no passing trade, and passing trade is vital. Yes, there is a certain client base, but that's diminishing rapidly because everyone, *everyone,* likes a bargain. People are shopping where it's cheaper. And don't forget the mail-order problem…just another headache for retailers.' He ran a hand through his hair. 'I know that this has been a wonderful family firm, and has done well in its day, but that day has passed. You can't survive on love, luck and thin air. Which has been what the Lewises have done for too long. Business is business, Cryssie. Dog eats dog in this world, and *profit* is what the world exists on!'

By now he was nearly as worked up as Cryssie, his voice rising sharply, and he turned away from her, irritated at her angry response and his own reaction to it. Of course he'd known from their very first encounter that she was intensely loyal to Hydebound, and to her colleagues, but if she thought that anything she said now would make him change his mind, she was fooling herself. When he set out to get his way he always succeeded, and nothing and no one would change that!

He saw that her shoulders had slumped, and her hand was

across her mouth to stop herself from crying. He broke the silence, which was heavy with tangled emotions.

'The reason I asked to see you,' he said, more quietly, 'is that I want to retain you as my personal assistant. It'll be hard work, which will take you away from home sometimes, and that may be a problem for you, but—'

'No, *thanks!* And I wish to hand you my resignation *now!*' Cryssie cried defiantly. 'I'm not used to working for *ogres*—however successful!' She marched over to the desk, looking frantically for something to write on, and he followed her, gripping her arm with a ferocity that frightened her.

'Stop! Don't be so ridiculous!' he said, raising his voice again. 'Hear me out—for God's sake, Cryssie, calm down!'

'Calm down? I've never been calmer in my life!' she retorted angrily. 'Just find me a pen and…the back of an envelope will do! I'm finished here! I'm the first one out!'

'No, you are not,' he said sternly, still gripping her tightly. '*Listen* to me! What you decide in the next few minutes may affect you for the rest of your life! I'm offering you the best chance you're ever likely to have! I want you to stay here and pour oil on obviously troubled waters until the last orders are completed. And after that to be my right-hand woman. And I'm trebling your present wages as an incentive.'

That last remark made Cryssie hold her breath for a split second. *Treble* her wages, had he said? To think of that sort of money being at her·disposal was the stuff of unlikely dreams. But her hesitation didn't last long! He was not going to buy her off like that!

She stared up at him, and by now they were so close that she could actually hear his heart thudding against his chest, matching the agonised throbbing in her own.

'Keep your job, Mr Hunter,' she said, trying not to shout. 'And keep your money! Money isn't everything in life.'

'It is in business, you little idiot,' he said, and suddenly his arms were around her waist.

He dragged her towards him, forcing his mouth over hers, the full weight of him almost making her knees buckle. Completely amazed, Cryssie felt her lips part in shock, and the moist warmth of his tongue against hers. And then there was no other sound in the room except the pounding of her heart in her ears. No other sensation except the awareness of his masculinity, the overpowering thrust of his body against hers, and after a split second's realisation as to the enormity of what was happening to her, all Cryssie's forthright determination seemed to desert her. To be held tightly, like this, was strangely comforting, even under these circumstances, subduing her volatile expressions of anger and resentment, and she automatically leaned into him, the smell of his hot flesh reaching her nostrils, arousing her senses so that for this particular moment in time she was, once again, under his complete control.

How long they remained in that very intimate position Cryssie could not afterwards remember, but eventually he released her, with a sigh that was more like a shudder, and held her away from him, visibly upset at his unusual lack of self control. When he spoke, his voice was harsh.

'I advise you, very strongly, to think carefully about what I'm offering you.' He drew his lips together in a forbidding line. 'I do not do such things lightly,' he added tersely. He didn't look away from her flushed face, and the green eyes that seemed to have become as wide and wild as a cat's. 'Don't be impulsive,' he repeated. 'I need you—not just here, for the immediate future, but for our other companies elsewhere.. I've been looking for someone for a long time—a woman with a head on her shoulders, a clear mind, and opinions she's not afraid to express. Do you understand what I'm saying?'

'Why don't you ask Rose?' Cryssie asked, trying desperately to keep a grip on herself, on her fluctuating emotions.

'Why should I want an over-made-up grandmother—a "yes" woman?' he demanded, and Cryssie was fleetingly surprised that he'd even noticed Rose's thick orange foundation and gash of red lipstick. 'I want someone to challenge me sometimes—perhaps to make me see things in a different light!' He shook his head angrily, annoyed that he was having to persuade her to see things his way. 'Women like you are rare. You're the person I want, and I'll make sure you have a good package.'

Cryssie listened quietly to all this, glad of the chance to reconnect with her self-control. Then she said, 'Well, so far I haven't managed to make you see things in a different light,' she said, trying to keep the sarcasm from surfacing.

'Cryssie—the Lewises were ready to file for bankruptcy. Surely *you* must have realised?'

Cryssie had to admit that she'd had no idea things were that bad.

'I've at least saved the brothers from that ignominy,' Jed went on. 'I've settled all their debts, including their tax and VAT, so they've been able to leave with their heads held up, because all the town knows is that they've sold out and retired. Perfectly natural after forty-five years of popular trading.' He looked down at her, waiting for her to say something. 'And,' he added, 'I've paid well over the odds for Hydebound, because it's the land that I'm interested in. It's a very valuable site, and it'll be money well spent.'

By this time Cryssie's role as provider for the family had reasserted its importance in her mind and she hesitated. 'So…you need me—' she began, and he interrupted her.

'Yes. And you need *me*, Cryssie.' He paused, ready with the knock-out blow. 'And Milo needs me. Or he needs my money. As I've said, you can count on a more than favourable salary for as long as you want it. Life will be easier—a lot easier—for the family. Doesn't that make any difference?'

It made all the difference! And they both knew it. Cryssie groaned. 'No one will ever speak to me again,' she said. 'When they find out that I'm the only one to be given future employment. How can I cope with that? We're all friends here!'

'You'll cope with it by not saying a word,' he replied evenly, now totally Mr Big, ready with all the answers. 'You'll be here for the next few months, as will everyone else, and there's no need for anyone to know a thing until the heat has died down. After that—well, who knows what will happen?'

'If the plans for the hotel go through—' Cryssie began, and he interrupted again.

'Oh, they'll go through,' he said at once, and Cryssie shot him a quick glance. Of course they would—if Mr Jeremy Hunter said so! 'The hotel will be up and running on this site in eighteen months—or less, if I get my way.'

You'll get your way, Cryssie thought. Mr Unstoppable!

But he was right about the most important thing in all this, and her common sense prevailed. She knew that for Polly and Milo's sake she couldn't refuse this once-in-a-lifetime offer. But she still could not fathom why *she* was his choice of personal assistant. There must be many whom he'd be proud to be *seen* with, who could provide exactly what he needed. Finally, she turned to look up at him, her mouth firm.

'Then…I accept your offer,' she said, in a tone of regret, and she watched the slow smile of conquest cross his elegant features. And that irritated her, because she knew that he had won.

'Thank you, Crystal…Cryssie!' he amended quickly. 'You won't regret it.'

'I sincerely hope not,' she said pertly. She hesitated. 'I'd better go, or Rose will wonder what on earth you had to say to me.'

Turning, she walked swiftly across the room and threw open the door—to find Rose standing there, transfixed, with a look of total incredulity on her face. A massive wave of horror swept over Cryssie as she realised that the woman must have been outside all the time. Help! She might easily have witnessed the physical encounter between her and Jed through the partially glazed door panel!

'What the *hell* was all that about?' the woman said. 'I couldn't quite catch all of it, but I saw… Did he *force* himself on you?'

'Well, hardly,' Cryssie denied, closing the door behind her. 'And what you saw was anger, Rose—total, uncontrollable anger.'

'What do you mean? What at?'

'Oh—at something I said,' Cryssie said quickly. 'I was totally out of order, and he couldn't take it. It was *too* much, coming from someone like me! What you saw was the typical reaction of some men when they're infuriated. They show their annoyance in that way to regain their self-belief. It's a male thing,' she added. 'He sort of pushed into me—pushed me away—that's all,' Cryssie went on, hoping that all this was making sense.

'It looked a bit more than that to me,' Rose said, throwing Cryssie a shrewd look. 'And if you want to take it further I'll be your witness!'

'It won't come to that,' Cryssie said at once. 'I don't hold with going to law at every opportunity. Anyway, it wasn't anything that would stand up in court.' She hesitated. 'Don't worry about me, Rose. I can look after myself.'

As she drove the couple of miles home, Cryssie's mind was in utter turmoil. Giving in her notice, and then being offered an unbelievable opportunity all in one brief hour was almost too much to take in. To say nothing of having felt herself engulfed in the heated, muscular embrace of her new boss!

Pausing at the lights, she glanced briefly at her troubled face in the mirror and heaved a long sigh. A sigh of unexpected regret. Because everything she'd tried to explain to Rose was actually a fact. She knew only too well that Jed's strong, passionate mouth on hers, the contours of his body melding with her own, had been exactly what she'd said it was: the result of his irrepressible anger. Nothing more and nothing less. And, despite all her good intentions, she knew that she was, once again, falling for a man she wanted to despise!

CHAPTER SIX ·

AT THE end of the following day, the news was broken to the rest of the staff. Standing in Jed's office, everyone listened with unbelieving ears as he spelt out his plans for Hydebound, his awesome presence stopping anyone from asking too many questions. As always, he was entirely in control. Cryssie kept her head down, her heart fluttering uncomfortably.

He left abruptly, and back in their own room, after several minutes of Rose giving her thoughts on the matter an airing, Cryssie said, 'It's unbelievable, Rose, and all that's given me a splitting headache. I'm going home early—do you mind locking everything up?'

Later that evening, after she'd put Milo to bed, Cryssie changed into her navy tracksuit and loosened her hair. She flopped down on the chair opposite Polly and, glancing at her sister, thought for the millionth time what a beautiful girl she was, with her long auburn tresses shining as usual, because despite her emotional problems, Polly took good care of her appearance. And her apparent frailty seemed to give her a certain allure, her large grey eyes always seeming too big for her face.

At around nine o'clock, Polly stretched and sighed, and glanced at the clock. 'I think I'll go on up, Cryssie.' She yawned, and Cryssie thought, Please don't tell me you've had a tiring day!

'I shan't be long either, Poll—I'll see if I can finish this crossword first. I can't bear to let it beat me.'

At that moment there was a discreet tap on the front door, and the girls looked at each other in surprise.

'Who on earth can that be?' Polly said, not attempting to get up. 'We don't get visitors.'

Cryssie got to her feet at once. 'There's only one way to find out,' she said. Leaving the safety chain in place, she opened the front door cautiously, peering through the restricted space, and gave an audible gasp as she looked up into the black, black eyes which seemed to dominate all areas of her life!

'Oh, J—Mr. Hunter...' she said, feeling her face burn with embarrassment and shocked surprise. 'What...is there something wrong?' Even her voice didn't sound like hers!

'No, no—nothing's wrong,' he said, in a tone which suggested that he thought it perfectly normal to visit a member of staff at this hour, and without warning! 'Cryssie...can you spare me a few moments?'

Cryssie's heart was hammering. What on earth was *this* all about now? Surely there was nothing more that could happen today?

'Of course.' She slid the chain off and opened the door. 'Come in,' she said, thinking wildly that their humble dwelling was not exactly the kind of place he would ever expect to set foot in, especially with the detritus of the day—discarded newspapers, toys still in evidence everywhere—littering the room.

As he entered, Polly got up from her lying-down position on the sofa and stared straight up into Jed's face—and her own was a picture! Cryssie's eyes flitted rapidly from one to the other, and she saw immediately the effect this handsome stranger was having on her susceptible sister. *Oh, no, don't come on to him, please, Poll! It won't work!* But what did *she* know? Because Jed's gaze had taken in Polly in one perceptive moment—the slight figure in tight jeans and flattering loose cream top, her hair draped carelessly over one shoulder, the haunted eyes glistening with interest. She was a desirable woman by any standards, and Cryssie knew it only too well. But in their restricted lives they never usually came across any man who would ignite Polly's inborn lust for male attention.

Clearing her throat, Cryssie said, 'Mr Hunter, this is my sister Polly…Poll, this is my employer, Mr. Hunter, who's just bought Hydebound. As I told you after Christmas.'

Polly slid herself gracefully off the sofa to greet the man, who took her small hand in his and looked down at her. 'I'm sorry to disturb you this late,' he said apologetically, and Cryssie detected the transparent admiration in his eyes.

Polly was working her old magic, she thought. And Polly was doing her own assessing, clearly bowled over by the man's penetrating black eyes, the uncompromising mouth and brilliant white teeth. He was wearing well-cut trousers, as usual, with an open-neck shirt and fashionable suede jacket.

He turned to Cryssie, who went crimson as their eyes met. She was only too aware that her own appearance was hardly eye-catching—the loose-bottomed tracksuit having seen better days and nothing on her feet, her tousled unbrushed hair hanging untidily around her slight shoulders. Then she forced herself to control her thoughts. This wasn't a competition between her and Polly for the benefit of Jed Hunter! If it was, her sister would win outright!

His voice broke the short silence. 'I'm sorry to barge in like this, but there is something rather important I need to discuss with you, Cryssie.'

Polly got up from the sofa. 'I was just on my way up to bed,' she said, smiling up at him, her cherubic mouth parted in the sweetest of smiles.

'Ah…' Jed said. 'I shan't stay long.'

Polly drifted out of the room, throwing a curious glance at Cryssie as she went, wondering why the girl hadn't bothered to describe her dashing new employer. She'd given an impression that he was old and bossy!

When they were alone, the two faced each other, and the reason for this unexpected visit suddenly dawned on Cryssie. Of course! He'd had time to think about his irrational behaviour in the office—and obviously bitterly regretted it! He might even have thought she'd make an official complaint, and he was here to apologise! This possibility had the effect of making her feel up-beat, and she drew herself up to her full height to meet his gaze. She was aware of the six o'clock shadow already darkening the strong features, emphasising the line of his jaw. She could also smell alcohol on his breath. It seemed odd, him being here in their pathetic little home, she thought, but he was as cool as ever, barely glancing at his surroundings.

'I was in the neighbourhood, having a drink with friends,' he said casually, 'and thought I may as well give you a call.'

'Oh—fine…' Cryssie said, waiting for the expected explanation for his earlier outburst.

'I've got business in London on Sunday—and I'd like you to come with me. You might as well start learning the ropes as early as possible.' His voice was flat and uncompromising.

'Sunday?' Cryssie echoed. 'Do people work on Sundays?'

He raised one eyebrow. 'Some do,' he said. 'When necessary. And Sunday is the only day one of my important clients has free. So I'm more than happy to comply.'

Naturally, Cryssie thought. Nothing stands in the way of big business...not in Jeremy Hunter's book. But she knew she'd have to agree. She wasn't in a position to obstruct any of his plans. Not at this early stage.

'Well,' she said rather reluctantly, 'I expect my sister and Milo can amuse themselves for once. Do we have to be gone all day?'

'Afraid so,' he said briefly. 'So don't make other plans. We don't want to be tied.'

For a second Cryssie felt like refusing to go along with his plans. It seemed a bit soon for him to be running her life—especially as she'd only just agreed to be his PA. But she wasn't in the mood for any more battles Not today.

She shrugged. 'What time must we leave?'

'I'll pick you up at ten o'clock,' he said. 'The meeting's at two, which will give us time for a bite to eat first.'

Cryssie bit her lip. The way she was feeling, the idea of a 'bite to eat' on a Sunday—the day she always reserved for cooking a proper roast lunch for the family—didn't sound very attractive. But there was no getting away from the fact that she'd promised—had been more or less forced to promise—to be Jed Hunter's personal and private secretary, so she might as well accept the fact and get on with it.

He made no effort to go, and after a moment Cryssie said awkwardly, 'Would you...would you like a coffee? Or do you have to be somewhere else?' The last part of her remark was made more in hope than expectation!

'No. I'm not going anywhere. And coffee would be good. Thanks.'

Together they went into the kitchen, and Cryssie put the kettle on and reached for two mugs. She was glad that she always made a point of clearing up after their evening meal, so at least it was tidy enough for Jed to sit opposite her at the table as she spooned some instant coffee into the mugs.

'This is cosy,' he remarked, glancing around him.

'It does us well enough,' Cryssie replied, wondering what he was really thinking. She could only imagine the splendour of *his* surroundings, and 'cosy' would not be an appropriate word! 'The house is a bit on the small side,' she admitted, 'and when Milo grows into a long-legged teenager it might be more difficult to accommodate us all.'

As they sat with their drinks, he said, 'Have you told Polly about our—your—future plans? Or that Hydebound is coming to an end?'

'That's not the sort of thing I discuss with Polly,' Cryssie said slowly, thinking privately how lovely it would be to have someone to come home to who would be interested in what she'd done all day. 'She finds it hard to be bothered with life outside these four walls, so I never mention anything.'

There was silence for a few moments. Then he said, 'She's a very beautiful woman.' He paused. 'How does she spend her time?'

'Doing nothing very much at all,' Cryssie replied. 'She has trained as a beautician, but she suffered postnatal depression after Milo was born, and finds it hard to stick at anything for long. So it's best for her to be here, seeing Milo to and from school, and for me to earn our keep.' She looked away. 'It works perfectly okay,' she said, 'and as long as Milo has everything he needs, both emotionally and physically, then I'm happy.'

As if on cue, a small face appeared around the door, and Cryssie looked up in surprise.

'Milo! What are you doing awake, darling?'

The child came over and immediately got up onto Cryssie's

lap. 'I had a bad dream. I can't sleep,' he said. 'And I heard voices.' He looked across at Jed, who grinned.

'Hi, Milo,' he said easily.

'Hi,' the child said, unabashed.

'This is Mr Hunter, Milo,' Cryssie said.

There was a pause. 'Is he your friend, Cryssie?'

Cryssie smiled as she kissed the top of the curly head. 'Yes, he's my friend,' she said, shooting a quick glance at Jed, whose dark eyes held her captive for a second.

After a minute, Milo said, 'Did Mummy tell you I want a new bike for my birthday, Cryssie?' he asked.

'She did, Milo. We shall have to see what we can do, shan't we? Perhaps we'll go to the shops at the weekend and see what they've got, shall we?'

'*And* I've got to have a proper school uniform,' Milo said importantly. 'Mrs Hobson told us this morning. I'll have to wear a tie!'

'Oh, you'll look so grown-up!' Cryssie said fondly. 'Don't get any bigger, Milo,' she added. 'I like you just as you are!'

The child snuggled into Cryssie as if he never wanted to let her go. 'Can I sleep in your bed tonight? I don't want to go back into my own room.'

'We'll see. You close your eyes now, and we'll go up in a minute.'

Milo did as he was told, and was soon breathing deeply as Cryssie and Jed sipped their coffee. Presently, the man said, 'What a beautiful child.' He paused. 'Am I allowed to ask who his father is?'

'No one really knows,' Cryssie replied. 'Even Polly's not sure, and she wasn't interested enough to pursue the matter at the time. Great-Aunt Josie, who practically brought us up, had died a year earlier, then Poll found out she was pregnant

and everything seemed to go pear-shaped at once. Anyway…'
She paused, burying her face in Milo's curls. 'What does it
matter now?'

Jed nodded slowly 'They're very lucky to have you,' he said.

'And I'm lucky, too,' she countered at once. 'I've got everything I need.'

He looked at her quickly. 'Not many of us can say that,'
he remarked.

The child stirred, and Cryssie said softly, 'I'd better get him
back to bed…'

Jed stood up immediately. 'Here—let me take him. He's
nearly as heavy as you, I should think!'

And with one easy movement he lifted Milo from
Cryssie's arms and let her lead the way upstairs to the diminutive but prettily equipped bedroom. Laying the child down
gently, he wrapped the duvet around his small shoulders.

'I notice he didn't wake his mother with his nightmare
problem,' he whispered, still gazing down at the sleeping child.

'No, I'm always the first to know about it.' Cryssie smiled.

Together, they went silently down the stairs and, after calling
a cab on his mobile, Jed stopped by the front door. 'Remember—
ten o'clock on Sunday. Don't be late,' he said abruptly.

'I'll be ready,' she said, her curtness of tone matching his.
How quickly he could change his mood, she thought. He'd
obviously liked Milo just now, and been interested in the little
boy. But now it was back to business.

They were standing so close that one tiny movement would
have brought them together. And, despite everything, every
pore in Cryssie's body exuded a longing, a crushing desire,
for him to hold her so tightly that breathing would be difficult—which it was at that moment!

Frantic with foreboding at the way her life seemed to be

heading—an emotional path, running down hill—she implored silently, Please go now, Jed! Please!

With a sudden strong movement he opened the door to let himself out into the night, and with barely a nod of his head he walked away down the path.

She watched him go before quietly shutting the door and switching off all the lights, then made her way slowly up the stairs.

But sleep wouldn't come that night, and she lay there, inert and confused. Confused at the realisation that Jeremy Hunter had reawakened her feminine desires in a way that terrified her. She did not want this—she did not *need* it! Not after all her good intentions! But her life was becoming horribly linked with Jeremy Hunter, and she felt trapped between their financial needs and her emotional dilemma.

Silently, in the darkness, the tears began to flow. Hot, wretched tears she'd not known for three years. Because she knew that the first man to kiss her for so long had done so in sheer frustration at her stubbornness. It had been nothing more than that. It was not desire, or lust, even—but white hot frustration that had driven Jeremy Hunter to momentarily overpower her. It was unthinkable that any woman should try to thwart the great man's ambitions!

Rolling away in the taxi, Jed found his emotions churning. Over recent years he had developed a secure and satisfying shell around himself which he was determined that nothing and nobody would ever break. He was safe, impervious, emotionally water-tight.

Yet ever since Ms Crystal Rowe had crossed his path he had been in danger of falling off the emotional safety net… She had an annoying habit of getting to him! He wouldn't easily forget the look on her face—a look of pure devastation—when he'd given her the news about his hotel plans.

He'd spent that evening alone at the pub, going over and over everything they had both said yesterday and much more importantly—remembering their unexpected clinch! What could he have been *thinking* of? He cursed under his breath, remembering his lack of restraint, but acknowledged that he had been gripped by something unstoppable. The fire in her eyes as she'd accused him of low behaviour towards Hydebound had lit a fire in *him*—a fire which had turned frustration into a boiling passion, however fleeting. He dwelt again on those few moments, and his lip curled slightly at the memory. Because he knew she had shared that passion. It had been all too recognisable! He had felt her melt into him unashamedly, just long enough for him to be acutely aware of it. And, however much she tried to portray herself as self-sufficient, determined, aloof, she was no disinterested female. That day the blood in her veins had run as hot and uncontrolled as his own!

CHAPTER SEVEN

ON THE following Sunday morning, Cryssie followed Jed along the heavily carpeted hallway of an imposing block of flats until they reached a door at the end. Going inside, he went immediately over to the huge bay window and pulled the expensive drapes back, to allow the wintry midday light to fill the corners of the room.

Cryssie tried not to let him see the expression on her face as she looked around. It was an obviously male abode, unfussy but opulent, furnished with a couple of sofas and a deep armchair, two or three low tables, and a massive flatscreen TV in the corner. A large gilt-framed mirror over the fireplace reflected the series of London prints on the wall opposite, and one or two valuable ornaments graced the ornate mantelpiece.

Jed threw his laptop onto the chair, and turned to Cryssie. 'This is my pad—my bolthole when I'm in London,' he explained briefly. 'It's a useful tool, and much more comfortable than booking in to dreary hotels all the time.'

'A useful tool' was hardly what Cryssie would have called it! 'It's very…nice,' she said, rather lamely. 'Obviously conveniently situated.'

'Oh, it's served its purpose over the few years since I bought it,' he said 'It's good for entertaining business associates from time to time.' He glanced at her. 'We'll go next door to Renaldo's for something to eat in a minute, but do you want to see around the place?' he asked. 'I know you women are interested in such things.' He went across the room. 'This is the bedroom—with small dressing room attached—and here's the bathroom, plus one airing cupboard, and over here, the kitchen.' He smiled down at her. 'I've only ever prepared coffee and toast here—oh, and a couple of omelettes, if I remember rightly.' He paused. 'When I entertain, the chef at Renaldo's, the bistro next door, usually does the honours. Sends everything up—no problem. Much less fuss all round.'

Cryssie was impressed. This must have cost a fortune. Then she shrugged inwardly. What did it matter? As long as he prospered, then at least for now her own chances were rosy! But she still couldn't help feeling uneasy at her situation. What was she letting herself in for? she asked herself, over and over again. Because she knew she wouldn't ever be able to trust the man. And—much, much worse—could she trust herself? She had to admit that sometimes her common sense threatened to be outweighed by her susceptibility to Jeremy Hunter, even though she was desperately trying to keep her distance.

He sat down and opened his laptop. 'There are one or two things I need to check up on,' he said, not looking at her. 'You make yourself at home.'

Cryssie went into the bathroom, glancing at herself in the long mirror on the wall and smiling briefly at her own appearance. Her simple black suit, bought many years ago, had stood the test of time. It had a classic cut and teamed with her ivory shirt, created an unfussy, neat look which she felt was perfect for today.

Polly had insisted on lending Cryssie her special earrings—large, round, faceted studs, which caught the light as Cryssie moved. And they did seem to add something special to the overall effect, she had to admit.

On their journey Jed had explained that the client they were meeting owned property which the Hunters wanted to buy. But apparently bargaining would be tough.

'What's my part in this?' Cryssie had wanted to know.

'Just to listen and take accurate notes,' Jed had replied. 'It's essential to have all the details on record. And I can't remember every single thing that's said.'

He looked up as she went back into the sitting room, his glance sweeping the length of her body. He liked her in that suit, he decided instinctively. It made her look discreetly attractive—and she had on some sort of funky jewellery which glamorised her dainty features. He'd love the chance to dress the woman, he thought, really spoil her. Then his face darkened. Those were dangerous lines to think along—he'd done that before, and look where it had got him.

Suddenly his mobile rang, and he turned away to answer it, his expression darkening as he listened. Watching him, Cryssie realised that she was beginning to read the man like a book. Something didn't please him!

'Okay—yes, I see… Well, thanks for letting me know.' He snapped the phone shut and looked over at Cryssie. 'That's a damned nuisance,' he said shortly. 'The client has gone down with some mysterious bug or other…so that makes today a complete waste of time, I'm afraid.'

He pursed his lips, clearly irritated, and Cryssie said quickly, 'Never mind—these things happen,' thinking that, *good,* they could go straight back home!

His brow cleared then, and he appeared to relax. 'We won't let the day slip through our fingers,' he said. 'After lunch we'll have a stroll along the river—perhaps go down to the

Serpentine.' He glanced out of the window. 'The sun's coming out, and it's not too cold…we may as well enjoy ourselves and salvage something from an abortive assignment.' He turned to look at her again, and paused. 'Do you think we could be two human beings, rather than the employer from hell and his reluctant employee?' he asked gravely, and Cryssie felt herself being helplessly swept along with his plans. 'It'll give us some time to get to know each other—to understand each other a bit more. If we're going to be working closely together we need to get close… If you see what I mean.'

Cryssie swallowed. Of course what he was saying made sense, and she smiled up at him quickly. 'I've only ever been to London once,' she admitted, 'and I'd love to walk along the Thames. You can point out everything to me as we go.' She was suddenly enlivened by the idea of a historical tour, a day out, and he seemed pleased at her words.

'Great,' he said. 'But a spot of lunch first, I think.'

Next door at Renaldo's they went down a long flight of stairs to a table set in an alcove. The rather dimly lit surroundings added a sensuous feel to the occasion—even at this hour of the day. Cryssie leaned forward, her elbows on the table, and cupped her chin in her hands.

'I can't really believe I'm here, doing this,' she said slowly.

Jed's dark eyes glinted in the half-light. 'Why—what's the problem?' he asked, knowing very well what she was talking about.

'Well, you know, everyone else at work is in a state of…shock—wondering what the future holds for them—and I'm, well…'

'Sitting pretty? Stop worrying,' he said roughly. 'Life's full of these ups and downs. You just go with the flow.' He poured them some water, darting a quick glance at her. She was a strange mixture, he thought to himself. Very mature in many ways, but in others unconfident and naïve. He was going to enjoy showing her around town, giving her a day off from family responsibilities.

They enjoyed a delicious pasta meal, and a bottle of Chardonnay, then took a cab to Trafalgar Square, which was crowded with sightseers, and hundreds of pigeons scattering everywhere to pick food up from the ground, before flying off in vast numbers at head height. Cryssie ducked anxiously a few times, and Jed looked down at her quizzically.

'These things don't bother you, do they?'

'A bit,' Cryssie admitted. 'I've always been afraid of anything that comes too close to my face.'

'Hmm…I must try and remember that,' he said enigmatically, and Cryssie coloured at the remark.

'Don't you have any hang-ups?' she asked. 'Most people do.'

'Nah…not really,' he said easily. 'Though I wouldn't volunteer to spend the night, alone in a room with a couple of poisonous snakes.' He grinned down at her. 'Do you want to do some window-shopping? Or some real shopping? There are bound to be most places open.'

'I'd love to walk down Oxford Street,' Cryssie said. 'But window shopping will do me fine.'

Strolling along the wide pavements together, in an afternoon which had become unusually mild, Jed kept wondering why he was feeling so—contented. So complete. The day was *meant* to have been about finalising an important business deal, not whiling away the time in a totally non-productive way. But he was enjoying himself! There were no pressures, no clients to convince, and he was getting a curious satisfaction out of Cryssie's delight in being here. Watching her as she stared at everything in the huge window displays made him wonder where she'd been all her life...she was like a child on Christmas morning!

Suddenly, he turned to see a tour bus bearing down on them and, grabbing Cryssie's hand, he made her trot behind him towards a nearby stop. 'Come on,' he said. 'You'll see more if we ride.'

Together they got on, and Cryssie went upstairs, followed by Jed, who pushed her along to the vacant seats right at the front. He could hardly believe he was doing this! *How* long was it since he'd been on a bus? Cryssie's excitement was infectious as they passed all the famous sights.

'I'm ashamed that at my age I've never seen all this before,' she said eagerly. She glanced out of the window. 'You obviously know it so well, it must be boring for you to spend time doing this, Jed.'

'I'm not bored at all,' he replied at once, knowing that he could sit in the corner of a corporation car park with this woman and not be bored! And for the life of him he couldn't explain it. He was conscious of the warmth of her against his shoulder and thigh as they sat there close, and he forced himself to edge away, giving them both some distance.

Presently the route was completed, and they got off the bus and began to stroll across one of the nearby parks, mingling with other couples and families who were enjoying the relaxation of Sunday.

'Uh-oh, I can feel spots of rain,' Jed said suddenly, glancing upwards, and within a few minutes they found themselves caught in a heavy downpour. 'Quick,' he said, shrugging off his casual jacket and covering Cryssie's shoulders with it.

'Jed—there's no need—' she began, but he silenced her.

'My shirt'll soon dry off—what you've got on will take

longer. Come on—let's run for it.' And together they made their way as quickly as they could towards the main road.

Laughing and gasping, they hailed a taxi and, sitting alongside her, Jed said, 'You won't want to be late getting back, will you? Back home to Milo…?'

With a start, Cryssie realised that she hadn't even thought of Milo, or Polly, or anything much else, for the last few hours. The thought came as quite a shock!

'Um, well, not too late, I suppose, Jed. Though I did say I didn't know when we'd be back,' she said.

He smiled to himself. 'Good, then we'll go back to the flat and maybe get Renaldo to send us up a meal later—unless you'd rather go out somewhere? There are plenty of smart restaurants I could show you.'

Cryssie looked up at him quickly. 'No—I'm happy to stay in,' she said. 'I'm feeling quite tired.'

The rain had caught them by surprise, and Cryssie's hair hung in wet curls on her shoulders, while Jed's was plastered thickly to his forehead. He ran his fingers through it, shaking his head like a dog, and Cryssie couldn't help laughing. 'Hurrah for English weather,' she said, and Jed grinned down at her.

He knew she couldn't care less about having her appearance mucked up, and he was beginning to realise that her total lack of vanity was a very appealing trait. He was not used to that kind of female!

They arrived back at the flat, and Cryssie flopped down on the sofa, half closing her eyes for a second or two. 'Wow,' she murmured. 'London's terrific—but tiring.'

Jed switched on several table-lamps, which gave the room a distinctly cosy glow, and glanced across at her. 'Do you want to lie down for a bit? There are a couple of phone calls I need to make, then I'll fix us a drink before we order our supper.'

Cryssie thought of that comfortable-looking bed, and suc-
cumbed! 'Just for five minutes, then,' she said, thinking that
he probably wanted to phone in private.

In the bedroom, she slipped off her jacket, skirt and shoes,
and stretched out on the soft covers. It was heaven! Letting
her thoughts drift for a moment, Cryssie found herself wondering just how many women had shared this bed with Jeremy
Hunter. He said he usually used the place for business
purposes, but it was obviously also ideal for bringing home
whichever female took his fancy at the time.

She opened her eyes lazily, letting her gaze wander around
the room. Strangely, it had a more feminine feel than the rest
of the flat, with satin cushions dotted about, and some dainty
pictures on the wall. Without really thinking what she was
doing, Cryssie slid off the bed and went noiselessly across to
the adjoining small dressing room. Carefully, she opened the
door to one of the fitted wardrobes—and her suspicions were
confirmed! Hanging there was a beautiful pink satin dressing
gown, and a pair of soft, fluffy mules, decorated with sequins,
lay carelessly on the shelf beneath.

Shrugging, Cryssie quietly clicked the door shut and climbed
back onto the bed. Jeremy Hunter had other reasons for acquiring this place—so what? she thought. He was a free man, and
anyway—*she* had no reason to care one way or the other!

She closed her eyes for a second, trying not to think about
the man at all. But with him just a few feet away it was easier
said than done, and she knew she was restless. But presently
her thoughts settled down and she began to relax…

On the other side of the wall Jed lounged in the chair, his
long legs stretched out in front of him. He'd ordered their
supper to arrive in an hour. He fingered the glass of whisky
he'd poured himself thoughtfully. Only time would tell

whether their association could reach a different level which would be acceptable to them both. Because he was coming to realise that he wanted that—more than anything he'd wanted for a long time. But could he change the mind of this woman who'd emphasised that she was not in the market? He ran a finger across his lip, then poured himself another whisky.

There was no sound from the bedroom and, putting down his glass, he quietly went across and opened the door—just wide enough to see Cryssie, fast asleep, curled up on his bed. Lying there in just her shirt and underwear, with her hair loosened in careless fronds on the pillow, she reminded Jed of that other occasion. But this time he had to admit to feelings of a different nature… He knew so much more about her now, and he sensed that there was much more to discover. Yet it came as a major shock to realise that she was actually capable of arousing him, and he cursed under his breath at his disturbed emotions as he let his gaze linger on her sleeping form.

He went right into the room then, and stood by the side of the bed. Suddenly her eyes flickered open and she sat up, automatically drawing the cover over her shoulders.

'Heavens! Did I fall asleep?' she asked.

'You did. And our meal will be up in about ten minutes. Do you feel like it?'

'Of course!' Cryssie slid off the bed, picking up her clothes. 'I'll be quick,' she said.

She went past him into the bathroom, her heart racing. As she'd opened her eyes she'd thought for a breathless moment that he was going to try and seduce her. Because there had been something in his expression, something in those smoulderingly black eyes, that had made her tingle with apprehension—or with something else! It was essential for both of them that she got fully dressed now, and back to official mode!

This was the perfect setting for a romantic liaison. She shuddered as she allowed her mind to run along these forbidden lines, then quickly completed what she was doing and went back into the sitting room to join him—just as the doorbell rang to announce the arrival of their supper.

He'd already set a table in front of one of the sofas, with cutlery and a couple of napkins and two wine glasses, and Cryssie stood watching as Jed allowed the waiter to bring in the covered dishes. It all smelt fabulous as the man placed everything in front of them, and Cryssie realised that she was actually starving!

When they were alone, Jed brought over a bottle of wine from the drinks cabinet and poured some into their glasses. 'It's been good today, Cryssie, even if the meeting didn't go ahead.' He looked at her broodingly for a second. 'Let's drink to the next time.'

Cryssie lowered her eyes as she drank, knowing that she had enjoyed every minute being with Jeremy Hunter.

The meal was fantastic, and they both ate hungrily. 'I'd love to know what this sauce is made of,' Cryssie said, scraping around the plate with her fork.

'Mmm—it's a firm favourite here. I've ordered it more than once for people I'm entertaining,' Jed said, pouring some more wine. 'And no one's complained yet.'

Cryssie leaned back and gazed across at him, feeling warm and comfortable, all her inhibitions deserting her.

'Who does the gorgeous dressing gown in the wardrobe belong to?' she asked casually. 'Or is it just meant for the woman of the moment?'

Jed looked at her blankly for a second. 'I didn't know there was one there,' he said.

'Oh, come *on!* This is your place! You *must* know what's

in it! There is a beautiful pink lady's dressing gown, complete with fancy mules. She must be very high-maintenance, Jed! It's fortunate you're so successful in business!'

Jed's face had hardened as she spoke, and Cryssie was suddenly afraid that she'd said too much—overstepped the recommended mark, let her barriers down. It was none of her business!

He strode out of the room, and she heard him open the wardrobe door in the bedroom, then bang it shut angrily. When he came back, the knitted brows were drawn fiercely together, and for a moment Cryssie felt startled. She'd upset him this time, and he was angry! And she knew what might happen when he became angry!

'I had no idea that thing was still there—' he began, but Cryssie interrupted.

'I'm sorry, Jed. It's nothing to do with me what you keep in your bedroom—or anywhere else for that matter,' she said.

He shrugged. 'I haven't opened that particular door for two years,' he said. He paused. 'It was my wife's wardrobe—mine's the other one. I didn't realise she'd left anything there. She obviously hasn't missed it,' he said sarcastically. 'She had about a dozen others to choose from, I seem to remember.'

Cryssie was staggered! His *wife,* had he said? That was news to her! *Why* had she opened that wardrobe! She should mind her own business and leave her boss to his! She cringed at her crass behaviour!

By now she had stood up, and he came across to look down at her. She could see a pulse beating strongly in his neck, and he thrust a hand through his hair in an agitated gesture. He moved over to pour himself some more wine. 'I was married to Ella for just over a year. Just long enough for us to really get to know each other,' he added savagely. 'But I'm

afraid our terms and conditions didn't exactly tally.' He drank
from his glass, his face becoming a picture of anger and regret
as he spoke. 'I've not seen or spoken to her since the divorce,
and it'll stay that way. The remaining contents of that
wardrobe will be given to a local charity shop tomorrow. I'll
leave a note for the cleaner.'

When she could find her voice, Cryssie said, 'Life would
be so much simpler if we could look into the future—see the
way ahead.'

On that point they would surely agree, she thought. How
many times she'd wished *she* could turn the clock back!

He looked down at her for a long, thoughtful moment, and
then, almost in slow motion, he reached out to draw her
towards him, circling her waist with his arm and pulling her
close. She didn't protest, or try to resist him, because she
knew instinctively that he was going to kiss her—and, yes,
yes, *yes,* she wanted him to! What harm could there be in one
sympathetic, empathetic fusing of their lips?

And then she was totally helpless, under his control, and
he was pressing his mouth on hers in a way that was both
tender and yet fiercely passionate. Not like that other time,
she thought, her head swimming with desire. This was a
dream moment like none other she'd ever experienced, and
she found herself drifting into a state of near semi-con-
sciousness, letting him take her over, his breath fanning her
flaming cheeks.

'Cryssie,' he murmured in her ear. 'I want you. I need
you…' And, almost lifting her from her feet, he half carried
her towards the bedroom.

Suddenly, as if a wake-up call had sounded, and remembering the last time he'd held her like this, Cryssie stopped
and dragged herself away from him. 'No!' She gasped out the

word as if it hurt her, and he stared down at her, his eyes blazing like hot coals of incandescent fire.

'*Why*, Cryssie?' He paused, realising at once that he'd jumped the gun, been in too much of a hurry. 'Don't spoil the day! It would be the perfect ending…' he murmured.

'You need to know, Jed, that I don't engage in short-term affairs—let alone one-night stands!' She paused, listening to her own heart thudding in her ears. How close she had come to repeating the past!

He reached for her again, and she knew he was going to use all his persuasive powers to make her change her mind. But for once she had the upper hand.

'I haven't forgotten another occasion, Jed, when you—' she began, and he interrupted breathily.

'Yes—and you drove me to that, Cryssie! I was so frustrated at your…idiotic stubbornness….'

'Oh, I was in no doubt as to your motives, Jed!'

'You just made me so mad at your refusal to…to see sense!'

'Well, I'm seeing sense now,' she said, moving right away from him, her legs trembling. 'And I really must…I want to go home now.'

As if by magic he asserted himself again. 'Then that's what we'll do,' he said flatly, as if what had just happened between them had been nothing.

Cryssie hoped he was fit to drive, because he must be over the legal limit, she thought. But she knew Jeremy Hunter wasn't likely to endanger either of their lives. *That* would upset his business plans!

A chauffeur-driven limo took them home in comparative silence, and she knew he was disappointed at her refusal to allow him to make love to her. But she was glad that she'd not given in to him! She'd proved to herself that she was in total control of her life—of their lives—hers, and Polly's, and Milo's.

Jed's mouth was firmly set as they sped along the motorway. He'd never been turned down by any female ever before, but somehow it didn't get to him as much as he'd have thought. Because he knew he'd have his way in the end. The woman had proved that she was no push-over, yet for those timeless moments he *knew* that she had wanted him as much as he had desired her.

He glanced across at her covertly, and his gaze softened. This was not going to be easy, he thought—but he enjoyed a challenge. A grim smile edged his mouth. His idea, concocted almost overnight, would suit them both. All he had to do was make her see his point of view!

Finally, they drew into Birch End Lane, and Cryssie opened her door almost before the driver had stopped the engine.

'Goodnight, Jed,' she said shakily. 'And—thanks for the—for the…ride…' she added enigmatically, getting out and slamming the door.

CHAPTER EIGHT

JED'S BRAIN had been working overtime as he wondered how he could find a legitimate excuse to be alone with Cryssie without raising any suspicions. He knew she was desperate for the rest of the staff at Hydebound not to know anything at all about her new position in his business life, so when he did call in at the office his attitude with her was always strictly cool and formal.

Since their day in London a few weeks earlier, he just hadn't been able to get her out of his mind, and he knew that he was becoming obsessed with the woman—or rather obsessed with the need to put his plan into action as soon as possible. Too much time was passing—valuable time that was being wasted! And all his instincts told him that he was letting things go off the boil. Because, in spite of her insistence that she didn't want the complication of a man on her scene, he simply didn't believe it. The heady memory of their few moments of closeness convinced him that she was sexually alive, and vulnerable. She was a sensitive, warm-blooded woman, and he knew enough about the subject to be certain he was right.

The other factor that was making it almost impossible for him to get her alone was that he knew weekends were a no-go area. She valued her time with the family too much. But he knew he must wangle it somehow, or he'd be back to square one.

Then, one Saturday morning, something unusual came up which made it essential that he should visit one of their properties—and even though he knew she wouldn't be too happy about it he was determined that she'd do as he wanted.

Down in the kitchen, Cryssie was making the first pot of tea of the day when the telephone rang. She heard Jed's all-too-recognisable voice and her heart leapt automatically. She was being forced to live two lives at the same time, she thought, and it wasn't easy! Her mind would keep going back to the moment when he'd almost succeeded in seducing her, and when she allowed herself to dwell on it—which she was honest enough to admit she regularly did—she could actually feel his lips burning into hers, could recall the strength of his arms around her. Yet at work she was having to act out another scenario altogether, and every time she had to face him—especially if others were there—her hands actually shook. Between a rock and a hard place seemed an apt description of her position, she thought, though Jed was very good at keeping *his* thoughts private! No one would ever guess what was going on behind those black mesmerising eyes.

'Cryssie?' he said now. 'Sorry to give you such short notice, but could you be spared for the day? I want you to go with me to Wales—I need to visit one of our hotels. There's a bit of a problem there.'

Cryssie frowned. Weekends were a time for housework and catching up on everything. And taking Milo out somewhere. 'Well—it is rather awkward…I'm usually up to my eyes in domesticity on Saturdays—' she began, but he interrupted.

'I'm sorry—but I need to sort this thing out, and we can't go on a week day because it would raise a few eyebrows, wouldn't it, if you left your desk?'

Cryssie had to admit that that was true, but she had hoped that her new job wouldn't really begin until after Hydebound had finally closed—which was now a mere two months away.

She knew straight away that of course she would fall in with the man's wishes—she had too much to lose if at this early stage she started making excuses. It was not such a big deal, after all. Polly would simply have to be persuaded to venture out and take Milo to the cinema that afternoon by herself—Cryssie had already bought the tickets.

'What time do we have to go?' she asked.

'Nine o'clock—that gives you a whole hour,' he added helpfully.

Swallowing her mug of tea, and grabbing a piece of toast, Cryssie quickly prepared a breakfast tray for Polly and Milo and took it upstairs.

'Poll—I've got to go out for the day. There's a meeting at work… Sorry—can you take Milo to see that film? I shan't be late home.'

Her sister opened one eye, and grunted her appreciation as breakfast was put down beside her. 'Okay,' she said sleepily. Then, 'There always seems to be something going on at work these days.' She paused, adding thoughtfully, 'Will Mr Hunter be at this meeting?'

'Oh—I—yes, of course. He's collecting me soonish, because we have to visit somewhere away, I believe.'

Polly sat up and glanced at Cryssie. After Jed's unexpected arrival at the house the girl had been unusually interested in Cryssie's working life—and especially her dashing new employer, wanting to know everything about him. Cryssie had made a point of answering all enquiries vaguely, as if she wasn't interested enough to give the matter much thought. 'Well, I'm sure you'll have a more exciting day than me,' Polly murmured.

Just then Milo wandered in, clutching his Runaway Rascal doll and Cryssie bent down and hugged him, explaining that she couldn't go with them to see the film because she had to go to work.

'I don't want you to go,' the child protested. 'Please, Cryssie, don't go.'

'I have to, sweetheart—but tomorrow we'll do something special. Perhaps we could go swimming, and then out for a pizza? Is that okay?'

At exactly nine o'clock Jed arrived. The one hour he had so reasonably allowed Cryssie to get ready had been sufficient for her to shower and wash her hair. She had dressed in her one really decent tweed skirt, and in the honey-coloured cashmere sweater that Polly had given her for Christmas—a purchase from Latimer's, where Polly loved browsing when she felt fit enough to go out. But the same fawn jacket had to do to complete the outfit—it was the only winter-weight coat Cryssie possessed.

They got into the car and set off. This thing didn't drive along—it glided, Cryssie thought. She couldn't help smiling to herself.

'Something amuses you?' Jed asked, glancing across at her briefly.

'I was just comparing this with the old car that dear Great-Aunt Josie taught me to drive in,' she said.

'Doesn't matter—as long as you passed your test.'

'I did. First time,' Cryssie said at once. 'Our great-aunt was a bit old-fashioned, but she knew a thing or two, and she passed a lot of it on to us…me.' She paused. 'We lived with her after our parents were killed in an accident. We were just children at the time.'

There was silence for a moment, then Jed said quietly, 'That must have been a very tough deal…I'm sorry…'

Cryssie shrugged. 'Well, you know…kids are resilient. And Josie was always kind to us.' She paused. 'I'm glad she was no longer around when Polly got pregnant.' She looked across ruefully. 'So, you see, all the worrying has been passed on to me.'

Jed didn't reply to that.

He cleared his throat. 'Did you manage to sort things out at home? Will Milo forgive me for taking you away for the day?'

Cryssie smiled faintly, and nodded. 'He's going to see the latest kids' film this afternoon, with Polly.' She turned to look at Jed, her chest tightening. His powerful masculinity exuded from him with every movement he made, and a tremor ran through her which she tried to stifle. She waited a few moments before going on. 'What exactly *is* happening today?' she asked, returning her gaze to the road ahead.

'Something I hope I'll be able to sort out,' he said. 'But I thought it might be useful for you to come along and look the place over—see the sort of enterprise I'm involved with for future reference.' He paused. 'I've been so caught up with things at Hydebound I'm afraid I've let one or two other matters slip, so I've got some catching up to do. I haven't had time to put in an appearance at this hotel for a bit, and I like to keep my finger on every button where possible.' He frowned impatiently. 'It's something to do with the staff, by the sound of it, and I could do without that at the moment. It's bad enough trying to make a decent profit these days, without blasted personnel problems.'

'Personnel are people—human beings with feelings,'

Cryssie said at once. 'If something's wrong, there's bound to be a good reason.'

'I know that,' Jed said, 'and that's what I'm hoping to find out.' He frowned. 'It can be difficult to get to the heart of a situation… People don't always say what they mean. To me, at any rate.' There was a brief silence, and then, without looking at her, he said, 'It's good you're coming with me today. And, by the way, I shall pay you your first new pay-cheque next week… Obviously it won't go through the office accounts at Hydebound.'

He turned to look at her, taking in her appearance in one swift glance. 'And today we'll drop down into Bath and visit a department store in Milsom Street—I know one of the buyers there—and purchase a warmer coat for you.' He paused. 'I noticed that you shivered just now, and the one you're wearing is—'

'Is not very nice at all,' Cryssie interrupted quickly. 'And I've had it for years. But when I see the price of them in the shops I can't justify spending that sort of money. This one is perfectly serviceable,' she added defiantly, 'and, since I'm not at all interested in fashion, the fact that it's not up to the minute doesn't faze me in the slightest.' She tried not to let her annoyance at his remarks show, but he'd better not think he was going to take over her life completely!

He glanced at the dashboard clock. 'There's plenty of time to shop before we go over the bridge,' he said casually.

Cryssie gave him a sharp look. So he didn't want to be seen out and about with her dressed as she was today! And if it meant forking out for a new coat it would be worth it to him, as a face-saving exercise. She pursed her lips to stop herself from making an ungracious retort as these thoughts filtered through her mind.

As soon as they entered the long-established store, Cryssie was aware straight away of the attention that Jed attracted. He strode in front of her towards the ladies' wear department, and spoke briefly to the first assistant he came across.

'Is Ms Fletcher in today? Would you mention my name— Jeremy Hunter—and ask if she could spare us a few minutes?'

Almost at once Ms Fletcher gushingly presented herself.

'Jeremy!' The voice was audible to everyone within fifty feet. 'Why didn't you ring to say you were coming? I'd have put out the red carpet!'

Jeremy smiled darkly at the woman, and planted a brief kiss on both her cheeks. 'Hello, Lucinda. Good to see you again.' He paused. 'My assistant wants to buy a coat to wrap herself in against this cold wind.' He glanced at his watch. 'Impress me—we've about forty minutes.'

Cryssie was amazed—and aghast—at the man's cheek… and at his influence! He'd not only told *her* and everyone else that she needed a new coat, he'd automatically assumed that she was incapable of choosing one for herself! But, even though this fact irritated her, she could hardly blame the man. Any dress sense she might once have possessed had been swallowed up with the passing of time.

She followed the woman to the changing room, and eventually a beautiful fine woollen coat of an Italian design and fabric was decided on, in a deep aubergine, with a cosy collar that could be pulled up around the face and neck. Cryssie knew it suited her as soon as she put it on. Lastly, she was told that a pair of black high-heeled leather boots were an absolute must. Surveying herself in the long mirror, Cryssie had to admit that she'd never looked as good in anything in her life.

Jed's quick appreciative glance at her as she went back said it all, and he reached for his wallet immediately—much to

Cryssie's embarrassment. She didn't want him settling her debts—especially as he'd told her that she would soon have plenty of money of her own in the bank!

Cryssie's jacket and sensible shoes had been put into a large bag, it having been assumed that the new purchases were to be worn straight away, and together Jed and Cryssie left the shop. Cryssie's head was in a complete whirl. Someone else was suddenly in control of her life, she thought. It wasn't an unpleasant change to be looked after for once, but she felt anxious and concerned. Who knew where all this was going?

Outside, she hesitated. 'Could we find a toy shop?' she asked, looking up at Jed. 'I'd like to take something back for Milo.'

'Good idea!' Jed replied at once. 'There's a place just around the corner.'

They spent longer in the shop than they'd intended, as Jed kept finding things to amuse him. Cryssie had already paid for the puzzle and book she'd chosen when he joined her at the counter with a computerized toy that made loud squeaks and buzzes every time he pressed the brightly coloured buttons.

'I haven't seen any of these in our stock,' he said, 'but I think Milo will like it, don't you?'

'Oh, yes…but you shouldn't, Jed. I think you've spent quite enough on us today.'

'Well, let's just say that I like giving people things,' he said casually.

'Well, all *that* tells me is that if you ever have a family of your own they'll be ruined!'

He smiled darkly at her. 'That's a possibility,' he agreed, thinking how well the new coat suited Cryssie's figure. It fitted provocatively over the hips, and the gently flared hem skimming her slim calves was seductive. And the colour—the colour was just perfect for her, he thought.

She glanced up and saw him staring at her. 'What's wrong?' she asked.

'Nothing. Nothing's wrong. Why should there be?'

She shrugged. 'I thought perhaps you were regretting buying me this coat...for which many thanks, by the way.' She paused. 'There was no need, Jed. I'll be able to treat *myself,* now, won't I?' She patted her side. 'It's got lovely deep pockets as well. In fact...it's probably the nicest thing I've ever possessed...'

He smiled down into her eyes, which were sparkling like a child's. He wanted to say that it was money well spent— but he didn't dare. He thought of her sense of pride and self-sufficiency. She'd probably had to grit her teeth, accepting such a gift from him!

Just before lunch they arrived at the large, imposing hotel, and Jed swept into the car park at the side. Quickly releasing her seat belt, Cryssie slipped off the new coat and boots and reached for the bag containing her own things, which she'd thrown onto the back seat.

'What are you doing?' Jed asked

'Oh, I never wear *anything* new straight away,' Cryssie said. 'I like to leave it on a hanger in my wardrobe, getting used to the idea of owning it, saving up the pleasure. It's just one of my many foibles,' she murmured.

He shrugged, plainly mystified, and presently they entered the building, to be greeted by a middle-aged man with gelled hair to whom Cryssie, for some reason, took an instant dislike. Jed introduced him as Kevin, 'My indispensable manager, who runs the place like a military operation. And this is Ms Rowe, Kevin—one of my new assistants,' he added.

'Mr Hunter—you should have told us you were coming!' the manager protested, and Cryssie realised at once that Jed had deliberately not given notice of his arrival.

'Oh, I didn't know I could make it until this morning—but I'd be grateful if we could go over one or two things for an hour, Kevin…and we'd like lunch first, please,' he said.

'Of course—the dining room is not full,' the manager said, 'and Max is the chef on duty.'

'Ah, Max…' Jed turned to Cryssie. 'Max is fully qualified, of course, but he's also proving to be an ingenious chef. I'm very impressed with the guy.'

'I hope he serves lobster and pigeon,' Cryssie murmured, out of Kevin's earshot, as Jed guided her towards the dining room.

As they ate, Jed found himself wishing fervently that they were here to enjoy themselves—perhaps go for a long walk later, then dinner, and maybe an early night! But that was taking wishful thinking too far! He had enjoyed the long drive in her company, and the easy conversation that had flowed. He found her uniqueness totally appealing. She was the proverbial breath of fresh air, he concluded.

Presently Jed went into the manager's office for discussion with Kevin, and Cryssie was invited to go off by herself for an unofficial tour of the hotel. As she wandered around she hoped that Jed was finding out all he wanted to know about the problem he'd mentioned, and that it wasn't going to take for ever to solve. She'd told him that she didn't want to be late getting home, but exploring another of the Hunter ownerships was proving quite interesting, she thought, as she wandered the long corridors.

Eventually she found her way back to the reception area—via one of the lounges, where she was offered tea—to find Jed just coming out from the office. And soon they were on their way back home.

'Did you manage to sort everything out?' she asked

'Well, I suppose it was a useful enough exercise,' he

replied. 'Though I didn't discover what, if anything, is going on behind the scenes.'

'Who told you that anything was?' Cryssie asked.

'Oh…didn't I say? I received an anonymous tip-off in the post this morning. That's why I wanted to act at once. But although I asked Kevin many searching questions, hopefully without arousing suspicion, he assured me that everything is "cracking along just fine"—his words. So perhaps the tip-off was just a bit of malicious nonsense after all.' He waited to overtake a lorry before accelerating sharply away again. 'Kevin's so good at everything,' he went on. 'Managers like him are hard to find.'

Cryssie waited for a few seconds before speaking. 'No one's indispensable,' she said. 'You'd probably find a good enough replacement if you had to.'

He glanced across at her. 'What makes you say a thing like that?'

'Well, while I was wandering around—and eavesdropping, I'm afraid—I overheard a discussion in the corridor between two of the female staff upstairs…'

'And?'

'I think you've got real problems, Jed.' She paused. 'Apparently your wonderful Kevin is having an affair—with Max's wife. She works there too, doesn't she? One of the waitresses? Well, poor Max is in the dark, and his wife is acting Lady Muck—not pulling her weight, and Kevin's always giving her time off, spending some of it with her in private. The atmosphere amongst the rest of the staff is understandably tense and resentful. Especially as they all seem to like Max—much more than they like Kevin—and don't want to see him hurt.' She glanced across. 'Your name was mentioned—plus the fact that they all know Kevin's your "golden boy"… No one's got the guts to tell you, because they're afraid of causing even more trouble. So there you have it. In a not-very-nice nutshell.'

She could see that Jed was gobsmacked at this piece of information. 'I can't believe it,' he said at last. 'Kevin's married—with four kids! The man gave such a good account of himself today—and of everybody else.' He whistled briefly through his teeth. 'I thought him trustworthy—in all respects. How wrong can you be?'

They drove in silence for a few seconds, Jed's brows knitted in the formidable way that Cryssie knew only too well.

He cursed under his breath. 'Well, that's a hell of a dilemma,' he said. 'I don't want to lose either Max or Kevin, but from what you've told me I've got to do something about this—and fast.' The strong mouth was set in a grim line, and Cryssie could understand what the women she'd overheard had meant about not wanting to be the one to pass on bad news!

'Everything was going so well there,' Jed went on. 'Who was it that said hell is other people?' he asked flatly.

'I don't know who said that,' she remarked slowly, 'but they have a point, don't they?' Yes, Jeremy Hunter, she thought. And if they thought about it, the entire staff at Hydebound would be looking straight at you!

After dropping Cryssie home, Jed made his way back to Shepherd's Keep, the family mansion, deep in thought. He wasn't too sure how to sort things out now—what a bloody fool Kevin was! And how would Max react when he found out what had been going on between his wife and the manager? This could mean an almighty upheaval all round.

Sweeping into the long drive, he sighed, feeling empty and frustrated, wishing with all his heart that he was not going to be spending the evening with his parents—who would naturally want to know what he'd been doing all day. It would have been great to be chatting things over with Cryssie, just the two of them. His brow cleared momentarily as he thought over their time together earlier. When she'd emerged from the changing cubicle in the shop he'd almost done a double-take. She'd looked beautiful, standing there waiting for his verdict.

He smiled to himself then, as he sat there with the engine switched off. He'd not been able, at first, to make out why she'd taken the new coat off in the car—but of course he should have guessed straight away! He knew that he'd made it impossible for her to refuse his gift, but when and where she'd be wearing it was to be *her* choice, not his!

CHAPTER NINE

THE FOLLOWING morning Polly decided that, as she'd had to entertain her son for the whole of yesterday, today it was to be Cryssie's turn.

'I feel quite tired,' she said as, still wearing her dressing gown, she watched Cryssie clean the grate and set the fire ready for lighting. 'So I'm going to have a long hot bath and give myself a makeover. You don't mind if I stay here while you take Milo out, do you, Cryssie? I just feel like a day spent doing absolutely nothing.'

'Of course I don't mind, Poll,' Cryssie said at once, privately thinking that a day doing nothing sounded rather attractive. But 'doing nothing' didn't mean not spending time with Milo, and being alone with her little nephew would suit her fine!

She was just getting herself and the child ready to go out when the phone rang, and Jed's voice throbbed across the wires. Cryssie sighed briefly. The man's intrusion into her life was becoming a habit!

'Cryssie? Um—I've been thinking… It's a superb day today—really warm for early April…so different from yesterday—and I was wondering whether you—and the family— would like to come over here and admire our spring flowers.' He paused. 'I feel bad, having used up half your weekend on business, and I thought you might appreciate a few hours in the country.' He hesitated. 'Milo could bring his football—there's masses of space for a kick-around.'

The rush of pleasure that swept over her took Cryssie by surprise. She would just love to visit Shepherd's Keep—the grand place the Hunters owned—and see how the other half of the world lived! But, much more than that, his suggestion that Milo might like to play in the grounds pleased her more than anything.

'Oh—that's very kind, Jed,' she said hesitantly. 'But I'll have to ask Milo—he thinks we're going swimming.' She looked down at the child, who was standing by her side. 'Swimming or football, Milo?' she asked. 'You choose.'

'Football,' Milo answered promptly. 'Are we going to the park?'

'Sort of.' Cryssie smiled. 'A different one—and one you'll like!' She spoke into the phone handset again. 'Milo thanks you very much and is pleased to accept,' she said. 'But Polly won't be joining us.'

'Okay—fine—I'll be over at ten-thirty.'

After she'd rung off, Cryssie told Polly about the arrangements for the day and wasn't surprised when her sister's face fell.

'Oh…I might have liked to come too—if I wasn't so tired,' she said. 'You must tell me all about it when you come home, and I'll come next time.'

Cryssie was glad that her sister would not be accompanying them. She didn't particularly want the girl getting to know Jed and becoming attached to him—which she knew was a distinct possibility. Life had enough complications at the moment without asking for trouble, she thought. It would be far safer for just her and Milo and Jed to spend the day together, and the thought of them as a threesome filled her with unexpected pleasure.

Polly was safely out of sight in the bathroom when Jed arrived. Cryssie shut the door behind them and they went down the path together, with Milo clutching his precious football and trainers. Jed automatically lifted the little boy into the car and fastened his seat belt.

'This is low for you, isn't it, Milo?' he said. 'Next time I'll bring a specially raised car seat for you to sit on, so that you can see out more easily.'

Cryssie made herself take a long, deep breath as she looked over her shoulder at the child. The small face was wreathed in smiles as they exchanged glances—he'd never been in such a car in his life! And Jed's last remark more than implied that this wasn't to be a one-off occasion! Forcing every negative thought from her mind, Cryssie sat back, determined to enjoy the day ahead. If only for Milo's sake. The little boy lived a very happy life—she made sure of that—but the male influence was obviously missing, and that did worry her when she allowed herself to dwell on it. Especially when, a few months ago, Milo had come home from a birthday party wanting to know why a daddy didn't live with them.

When they arrived at Shepherd's Keep, Cryssie had difficulty in not gasping out loud. The fine Victorian building was grand enough, but as they drove around the curved driveway the grounds were a mass of crocuses, daffodils and narcissus, which swept across the lawns in wave after wave of sunny colour.

'Oh, Jed,' she whispered. 'This is…magical!'

He grinned across at her. 'I thought it might appeal,' he said. 'We'll walk across the field to the river later—but first we'll have coffee, and you must come and meet my parents.'

Cryssie bit her lip. She hadn't expected to meet the Hunter

family—not yet, anyway—and was relieved that Shepherd's Keep was well away from town and the possibility that she might be seen with Jed by any of her friends at Hydebound. Despite her pleasure at being here with Milo, she couldn't help feeling disloyal—and dishonest too. This time next year it could all be different, but for the moment the situation was too raw for comfort, she thought.

They went into the house through the vast kitchen, where Megan, the elderly housekeeper, was preparing lunch, and Jed introduced Cryssie briefly as they passed.

'I'll bring coffee into the garden room in a few minutes, Jed,' Megan said, smiling at Cryssie and Milo.

Surrounded by the Sunday newspapers, Henry and Alice Hunter looked up as Jed came in, followed by the others. Cryssie was instantly put at ease by the older couple, who greeted her in a very friendly way. They almost pounced on Milo, who was looking adorable in a fashionable little boy's outfit, his chubby face and golden curls shining with health.

'Do come in, my dear,' Alice said, getting up. 'Jeremy has told us about you…and this is Milo! What a beautiful child!' Alice Hunter was a smart woman, obviously no longer young, but with strong grey hair brushed up into a chignon, and quizzical blue eyes which twinkled as she spoke.

Henry, tall and distinguished-looking, stood up too, and came over to shake Cryssie's hand. 'So this is Jeremy's new assistant—glad to meet you, my dear,' he said, gazing down into her eyes, and Cryssie could see immediately where Jed's black ones originated! The two pairs were replicas, and as he held her hand for longer than was actually necessary the girl instinctively recognised Henry as a ladies' man.

Megan came in then with the coffee, and a glass of juice for Milo, while Cryssie surreptitiously glanced around her.

What on earth must Jed have thought of *their* place? she wondered, and suddenly she felt lost and out of her depth. She didn't belong here, with this fabulously wealthy family… Being employed in their office was one thing, but sitting drinking coffee and being made to feel so at home unnerved her. She was like a fish out of water, she thought helplessly.

But Milo had no such hang-ups, and, encouraged by Alice and Henry, was chatting away telling them all about school, and his toys, and the things he liked to do. 'Jed's going to play footie with me in a minute,' he said. 'Aren't you, Jed?'

Cryssie was surprised at the child's easy familiarity. There was no shyness or hanging around her—as he sometimes did when strangers were around. Milo had made himself quite at home, and was clearly enjoying all the attention he was getting.

'Yes, we'll go outside in a minute,' Jed said, ruffling Milo's curls. 'And afterwards would you like to see my train set, Milo?'

'Yes, *please!*' Milo said at once, and Alice smiled across at Cryssie.

'I'm afraid we can't bear to dismantle Jeremy's beloved train set,' she said. 'It's permanently set up in one of the spare rooms—to give it some use Megan's four grandchildren come over and play with it from time to time.' She paused and looked across at her son. 'And when no one's looking I'm sure Jeremy gets it going now and then,' she said fondly.

Cryssie didn't look across at Jed as she listened to what Alice was saying. It was difficult to imagine the masterful Jeremy Hunter on the floor playing with his toys!

Fortunately, the Hydebound question didn't arise in the conversation, which pleased Cryssie. She wanted to forget all about work today and concentrate on enjoying herself, and seeing that Milo had a good time. So, presently, the three of them went outside, where Jed and the little boy started to play an enthusiastic game of football while Cryssie admired the thousands of spring flowers that carpeted the lawns.

Wandering around in the surprisingly warm sunlight, and hearing Milo's shrieks of delight from nearby, Cryssie felt an almost overwhelming sense of sadness. For herself and for Milo. Here, there was everything that anyone could possibly wish for—a perfect place for a child to grow up. But she could never match it—hard though she tried to get everything right. Milo *needed* a man's influence, she thought miserably. Not just for things like playing football, but for the deeper, more important things in life. The years were flying by, and before they knew it Milo would be growing up and away from her. Would she be able to cope then, and with all the teenage problems that were bound to occur?

Although it was not cold, she shivered suddenly, and went back to join the others, stopping for a second to take in what she was seeing. Tall, elegant, and sophisticated Jeremy Hunter was throwing himself across the grass to stop her little five-year old from kicking the ball between the makeshift goal-posts they'd erected! But she reminded herself that this was not the only time she'd seen the man in a less than businesslike position… Her mental picture of him stretched out on the bed, wearing nothing but a pair of boxer shorts, refused to go away!

'You must pick some daffodils to take home with you later,' Jed said as she came up to them. 'And I'm fed up with playing with Milo, because he's scored more goals than me.'

Milo, hot and breathless, ran up to Cryssie. 'I like it here,' he said. 'It's fun. Can we come again soon, Cryssie?'

'Of course you can,' Jed said, answering for her. 'In fact, I shall insist on it!' He threw a glance at Cryssie, and for the millionth time his eyes held her captive and sent her blood rushing. He looked younger than she'd ever seen him, his hair tousled and damp, his wide brow moist with exercise, and when he suddenly scooped Milo up and put him on his shoulders to go back into the house she almost burst with an indescribable feeling of happiness. Milo was having a fantastic day! And so was she!

Presently it was announced that lunch was to be eaten in the kitchen.

'We usually have it here in the middle of the day,' Alice explained. 'It's cosier, and more convenient for Megan, rather than taking everything into the dining room.'

They all sat together at the long wooden table and began to enjoy the beautifully cooked lamb and spring vegetables. Milo ate every last scrap of his, to Cryssie's relief. He usually ate most of what *she* cooked for him, but you could never be sure that he would like someone else's cooking, she thought. And when ice cream and hot chocolate sauce was presented for pudding, the little boy's eyes shone even brighter.

'I didn't think Milo would necessarily appreciate apple pie,' Alice said, as she cut Cryssie a generous slice. 'But ice cream is usually safe. Megan's grandchildren eat here sometimes, when she has to look after them.'

Cryssie smiled her appreciation, thinking what a lovely family this was. Moneyed they might be, but pretentious they certainly were not. They seemed as ordinary as anyone else, liking the same things as everyone else. It was perseverance and hard work that had brought them to their position in life, she thought.

Glancing up, she saw Jed looking at her, and he gave her the merest wink as their eyes met. She'd love to know what he was thinking, because their relationship—such as it was— seemed to be taking more twists and turns than a rollercoaster. What on earth was she doing here, lunching with the Hunter family, in their vast home? And what was she doing here with Jed, the employer from hell, the destroyer of people's careers and hopes? And none of it was *her* fault! No one could say that she had manoeuvred herself into this position!

After lunch, Milo followed Henry happily upstairs to view the extravagant train layout. It surprised Cryssie that he didn't insist that she go as well.

'See you later, Cryssie,' the child said, as he left the room holding Henry's hand.

Jed pushed back his chair. 'Come on—let me show you around,' he said, 'while my mother has her usual post-lunch forty winks!'

The gardens were far more extensive than they'd appeared, and soon Jed and Cryssie had lost sight of the house altogether. Presently, they came to a small wooden lodge, built between the trees, and Jed pushed open the door for Cryssie to go inside.

'I used to have picnics here with my friends—after we'd skinny-dipped in the river,' he said. He sighed. 'But those days are past, sadly. No one uses this much any more—though the gardener has left some tools here, I see.'

It was a charming structure, facing downhill towards the river, which was just visible through the trees, and it contained a small, strong wooden table, a couple of deckchairs, and a two-seater swing chair. Jed sat gingerly down on one side, and patted the seat beside him for Cryssie to sit as well. 'I think it's still in good enough nick to hold our combined weight,' he said. 'Well, *my* weight,' he added.

Cryssie sat down as well, and leaned her head back. 'This is such a beautiful place, Jed,' she said quietly. 'You were very lucky to be brought up here.'

'I was,' he agreed. 'Though I don't think I realised it at the time. I was always allowed to bring my friends here—it was a fun time for me.'

They were so close that Cryssie could feel his strong thigh against hers, the warmth of his flesh mingling with her own. She ran her tongue over her lips, aware that her pulse had begun to race, and to break the spell that he always seemed to cast on her when they were alone she said, 'Have you decided what you're going to do about the manager, the chef, and the chef's wife?' she asked lightly, and he frowned, his mood changing in a second.

'I was hoping for some input from you about that,' he said seriously.

Cryssie was surprised that her opinion meant that much to him, but she said without hesitation, 'I'd have both Kevin and Max's wife in, together, and tell them that this affair must stop—now. Or they'll both be *out*—with no reference for them to give any future employer. You told me that Kevin adores his four sons, so he has a great deal to lose if his family splits up—and I doubt whether he'd ever get a salary to match the one you're paying him. The same goes for the wife. She must behave herself or she goes.'

Cryssie sat forward a moment, clasping her hands around her knees.

'Of course, that strategy may not work if they're deeply in love—but I very much doubt that is the case. From my impression of Kevin lust, not love, is the operative word, and Max's wife—obviously a much younger girl—has had her head turned by an older man. She'll get over it. And with a bit of luck poor Max may never be any the wiser—if it works out.' She leant back again, looking up at Jed, who hadn't taken his eyes off her as she'd been speaking. 'Don't blame me if you take that course and they end up resigning because they can't live without each other, though,' she added. 'That's a risk you'll have to take, and then the scenario for you will be having to find a new manager and waitress.'

She paused, frowning slightly. 'The most important thing, Jed, is the goodwill and contentment amongst the rest of the staff—and from what I was told that's in short supply at the moment. This very serious undercurrent can't be allowed to go on—it's undermining the running of the hotel, and the people who will soon be affected by this are your visitors. The ones who use their credit cards.'

'What if the two culprits go to law claiming unfair dismissal?' Jed asked.

'They're not likely to do that, are they?' Cryssie said. 'Because then the whole business will become public property. Anyway,' she added, 'if they do, you can settle out of court... A few thousand each won't hurt you, will it?'

Fixing her attention on matters of business had cleared Cryssie's mind of other things for a moment, and she stretched her arms above her head to run her hands through her long ponytail while she thought over what she'd just been saying. Turning to face him again, she said, 'But of course that's only *my* opinion...'

Instinctively he moved even closer to her. 'But that is exactly what I asked you for, Cryssie,' he said slowly. 'It's what I'll be paying you for...it's what I *need!*'

She looked up into his eyes, a slight frown clouding her expression. She wished that she could reach right into the mind of the man, really interpret what was going on behind those expressive eyes, she thought. What did he *really* want from her that he couldn't find elsewhere? she asked herself honestly. Because there was nothing special about her, and never had been. She'd been aware of that for most of her life.

As for his seduction attempt the other day in his flat—she knew that that counted for absolutely nothing. That sort of passionate incident was obviously normal routine for his type—relevant only to the passing moment, easily discounted and forgotten.

'Cryssie! Cryssie!' Suddenly Milo's voice broke the brief silence between them, and Jed cleared his throat.

'Anyway—thanks for your advice,' he said. 'I'll let you know what I intend to do, but we may have to go over there again at some point.'

Standing up quickly, they went outside, where Alice, Henry and Milo were strolling towards them. The little boy ran up to Cryssie.

'Jed's got an ace train set,' he said. 'I was allowed to work it by myself!'

'That's lovely, darling,' Cryssie said, smiling down at her little nephew.

Together they all wandered down to the river, where Milo's attention was soon taken up by finding small stones to throw into the water.

'He's having such a lovely day, Mrs Hunter,' Cryssie said, glad to have someone else to talk to for a minute, and to disengage herself from her employer and his tactics. She was aware of feeling unsettled—again! 'Thank you so much for inviting us,' she murmured.

'Oh, I hope you'll come often, my dear—and do call me Alice,' the woman added.

They sat down together on a grassy boulder a little way away, while the men watched Milo, and Alice said, 'The house is much too big now for Henry and me, of course. It was different when Jeremy was a child, and all his friends came to stay and to play. But the place—and the grounds—needs children. It's a family home, not a residence for the elderly!' She turned to smile at Cryssie. 'But that's *our* problem!' She paused. 'Jeremy has spoken so well of you—he says you're the first intelligent woman he's employed to date!'

'Oh, that's nice,' Cryssie said, feeling embarrassed at the older woman's words. 'I hope I shall live up to that!' She looked away for a second. 'You must be very proud of him, Alice.'

'Oh, of course we are—but he took rather a long time to grow up, you know! And that was our fault, of course. An only child, and we gave him the best of everything.' She was silent for a moment, lost in her own thoughts. 'It's not good to be an only child, you know,' she went on. 'To develop properly, to learn about life, there should be siblings to spar with, to share with, to match up to. And that's what we didn't give him. We always meant to, but we were so caught up with our various business interests it never seemed the right time. And before we knew it it was too late!'

She shook her head briefly. 'We spoilt Jeremy, and never expected too much of him, so he did spend a long time having too *good* a time! But since my husband was diagnosed with a heart complaint he's changed overnight—it's quite incredible. He takes virtually all the responsibility now for our businesses—which is a great relief. There does come a time when one must take a back seat. The work is hard, tiring, and relentless.' She patted Cryssie's knee. 'I know he's been on the look-out for a good assistant for a very long time, so we're grateful that he seems to have found one at last!'

The two women chatted amiably for a while, and Cryssie explained something of her background, and of her fears, to Alice, who was a thoughtful listener. But soon the sun went in, and Cryssie smiled, glancing at her watch. 'We must be going home soon,' she said gently. 'I know Milo won't want to leave, but my sister Polly will be expecting us at teatime.'

'Oh, must you go so soon? It's been so nice having a young woman to chat to, and hearing a child's voice in the place!' Alice said.

But presently they took their leave of Alice and Henry, and Jed walked slowly back with them to the car.

'We've had a fantastic day, Jed. Thanks,' Cryssie said simply, looking up at him.

He didn't reply for a moment, but watched as she strapped Milo into the back seat. 'I really must have a meeting with you soon, one to one, Cryssie,' he said. 'Perhaps it would be best for us to go to the London flat, where we can discuss things uninterrupted?' He looked away for a second. 'Find an excuse to have Thursday afternoon off. I'm free that day,' he added abruptly.

Cryssie got into the car and shut the door, looking up at him through the open window. 'I'll do my best,' she said slowly. 'It may be difficult, but I'll try and manage it somehow…' Then, with a brief nod of her head, she looked away, suddenly anxious at the coldness of his request, but knowing that of course she would do exactly as instructed!

CHAPTER TEN

CRYSSIE couldn't help feeling a warm glow of contentment. While she had to admit that *she'd* really enjoyed every minute of her time spent with the Hunters, it was Milo's obvious delight which had pleased her the most. Together with the undeniable fact that she couldn't help *liking* the wretched Mr Jeremy Hunter!

When they got home, she was surprised to find that Polly had gone out. A note on the kitchen table announced that the girl had taken herself off into town for a couple of hours. Cryssie was just tucking Milo up for the night when Polly returned.

'Hi, Poll! Where have you been? The shops are long shut. I was getting worried!' Cryssie teased.

'Oh…just wandering around town for a bit,' Polly remarked casually, going over to the bed to give her son a kiss. 'Did you have a good time?'

Cryssie gave her a brief outline of their day, with Milo chipping in enthusiastically, and presently the two women went downstairs.

As soon as they were alone Polly suddenly burst into a flood of hysterical tears, slipping down onto the floor and covering her face with her hands. Full of alarm, Cryssie crouched down beside her to hold her tightly. 'Whatever is the matter, Polly?' she said desperately. 'What…what on earth *is* it?'

Between gasps and sobs Polly poured her heart out to Cryssie, who could only sit there in a state of unbelievable shock as she listened. It was difficult to take everything in, to make sense of it, but eventually a cold rush of apprehension flooded her body. What sort of reaction was *this* going to get in certain quarters?

She let Polly go over and over everything for a solid hour, before she finally felt able to go and make some tea for them both, while promising her sister that somehow she would make things right. As she stood waiting for the kettle to boil Cryssie couldn't believe that such a happy day could end so disastrously. She buried her face in her hands. Once again, it had all landed in *her* lap!

As Jed had instructed, Cryssie arranged to take Thursday afternoon off. Thankfully, Rose had readily accepted Cryssie's excuse of a personal appointment with her bank, and soon she was once more sitting next to her employer on the way to London, feeling depressed and anxious.

The predicament that Polly had presented them with was proving to be an almost unbearable burden to her, and Cryssie knew that it would change everything. Obviously it would mean the end of her association with the Hunter dynasty. That was a foregone conclusion. She shuddered as she recalled Sunday evening and Polly's histrionics. She hadn't managed to get much sleep since. But she'd decided that today would be the ideal opportunity to draw everything to a conclusion. Whatever the very important business reasons Jed had for insisting they have this time together, nothing was more important than what *she* had to say to *him*.

They arrived at the flat by mid-afternoon. 'Make us a cup of tea,' Jed said casually, glancing at some mail that had been left on the table. 'You know where everything is.'

Obediently Cryssie went into the kitchen and quickly found everything she needed, filling two mugs and taking them inside.

Jed was standing by the window, his hands in his pockets, and as Cryssie handed him his tea she was struck by the expression on his rugged features. There was obviously something very important that they had to go through, she thought.

He put his tea down without tasting it, and said flatly, 'I want us to have a serious discussion.' He was choosing his words carefully. 'I want a more…shall we say—established agreement than we have at present,' he began, and Cryssie frowned. She didn't know what he was driving at—but anyway it didn't matter now.

He came across to stand close to her, forcing her to look up at him. 'I want you to link yourself more…personally…with me,' he said slowly, and when she continued to look mystified, he went on, 'I'm talking about marriage, Cryssie. And don't look like that! Are you so blind that the thought has never crossed *your* mind? Most women would have thought of it by now!'

Cryssie was staggered—and she almost did! She put her tea down and steadied herself against the back of the sofa.

'I'll spell it out for you,' he went on. 'I've been thinking about it for some time, and I believe it would be the perfect solution for both of us—mutually convenient in every way. Don't you get it? I want you *when* I want you, not just between the hours of nine and five. I need your good sense, your loyalty, your perceptiveness, your dedication. If we live together under the same roof it'll make things run more smoothly, more efficiently. I'll have everything I need—and *you'll* have everything you'll ever want or need for the rest of your life.'

Cryssie suddenly found the ability to speak, but when she did her voice was more of a croak! 'You're my *boss,* Jed,' she said, trying to add firmness to her voice. 'Business and… personal…relationships should be kept strictly apart!'

'Precisely,' he said smoothly. 'I've always avoided engaging in any relationships with members of staff—'

'But surely what you've just suggested—?'

'You won't *just* be a member of staff, will you, you little fool? You'll be my wife! You'll become one of the Hunters!'

Cryssie swallowed, reeling from this latest onslaught on her emotions. 'I'm sorry, but for me, the only acceptable aspect of our relationship is the formal one.' She shook her head. 'Have I got to explain everything to you *again?* Polly and Milo are utterly dependent on me. They are my life. I can't afford to think of anything or anyone else!'

'Oh, no?' He reached forward in one swift move and pulled her towards him, covering her mouth with his. 'I think I'm beginning to know more about you than you know about yourself…' he said softly.

Gathering her strength from somewhere, she pushed him away. 'No, Jed. You don't understand. I…'

'Oh, I understand perfectly,' he said huskily. 'You rather enjoy your life of martyrdom, don't you, Cryssie? There's a certain safety in what you have, with no emotional interruptions or commitments, no man to share your existence with. Yes, your sister and her son need you—but you need *them,* don't you? You enjoy their reliance on you. And what I'm offering you is the best of all possible worlds! You'll do yourself a big favour—and them too. There's plenty of room for them at Shepherd's Keep—they'd have their own part of the house, the run of the gardens—it would be their home! Surely you can see all the advantages? See what a practical, sensible thing it would be—for all of us?'

He released her slightly, waiting for a response. Looking up at him helplessly, Cryssie thought, Well, that was my first proposal of marriage. But *what* a proposal!

Suddenly her mind cleared, and she said coldly, 'What you've just accused me of—that I'm a martyr to the family cause—is true to some extent, I suppose, Jed. But I do have an even deeper reason for wanting nothing to change.' She took a deep breath. 'I was employed by someone once who was almost a carbon copy of you—in fact in some ways you could be blood brothers.' She looked away, knowing that he was staring at her intently. 'And do you know what? I believed that man—believed every promise that he made. But when something happened to make me see how close I was to ruining my life I got out. Fast.' She swallowed. 'You accused me of being blind just now. I was certainly blind then! And it made me realise that my true happiness will only ever be found with my family. Where I am, where I'm rooted. Where I can trust. And so far nothing has happened to make me change my mind.'

He shrugged then, and his lip curled. 'You're misguided, Cryssie. Take my word for it. The years will fly by, and there'll come a time when Milo won't need you—he'll be off living his own life. And you'll have given up half of yours! You'll be redundant! And what then? Will you look around for someone else to nurture?'

Cryssie was stung at his words, even though she knew he was right about Milo wanting his independence one day. 'My sister will *always* need me—' she began.

'Don't count on it!' Jed replied quickly. 'She's a beautiful, glamorous woman. It'll only take the right man to come along one day—someone who will understand her needs. Anyway...' he picked up his mug of tea and drank '...you'll obviously want time to think over what I've put to you, but be careful. This could be a turning point in your life that may never come again.'

Cryssie felt like bursting into tears. How could he think that she'd *ever* accept such a proposal? That she would agree to a marriage of convenience? And it was his *own* convenience that was uppermost in his mind! The word 'love' had been conspicuous by its absence! He clearly saw her as a good business deal, that was all! And although she never really expected to marry, if it ever did happen it would be for love! And to someone who needed her as a loving partner, not a live-in PA!

The last few minutes had almost bowled her over, but she found the strength to pick up her tea and take a sip, even though her hands were shaking. Now it was her turn!

'There's something else we need to discuss,' she said quietly. 'Something very serious.'

She looked up at him. 'Have you been in to the store—to Latimer's—this week?'

He frowned. 'No, I haven't. I've been caught up elsewhere. I've been ringing in, of course, but my managers are more than capable of holding the fort. Why do you ask?'

Cryssie's mouth dried. 'You've not heard anything about any…stealing?' she said hoarsely.

'Stealing?' he repeated curiously. 'Why on earth should you ask that? There've been a couple of incidents of petty pilfering, I believe. That's all. Nothing important.'

Cryssie took a long, deep breath. 'I'm afraid it *is* very important, Jed,' she said. 'Because it concerns Polly.' She looked away for a second, biting her lip, knowing that the words she was going to utter would hurt her like a knife wound. 'Polly stole a scarf—an expensive scarf—on Sunday…' Now the words came quickly. 'She was admiring a rack of them that they've got by the main entrance door, and in an act of total and utter stupidity she slipped one of them into her bag.' Cryssie took another desperate sip from her mug. 'Of course, the security guard saw her, stopped her, and warned her that she might face prosecution. She's threatened to kill herself if she ever has to go to court.' She looked up at Jed, her eyes filling with tears. 'And the thing is, she wanted the wretched thing for me, not for herself. It was to be a present for *me*.'

There was a moment's complete silence as Jed took this in, then, 'Your poor, poor sister,' he said quietly. 'How utterly traumatic for her.'

Cryssie was amazed at the kindness of his remark. 'How can you say that?' she asked shakily. 'She stole…actually *stole* something. And was caught!'

'Because Polly is in need of help—of support,' he replied grimly. 'She obviously lost all confidence after Milo's father took off, and she must feel so unwanted, so ineffectual—especially with a sister like you as an example of what she *could* be worth. Doing something completely out of character is typical behaviour for someone who needs consolation and reassurance.'

He shook his head, and Cryssie could almost—but not quite—have thrown her arms around him. She would never have credited Jeremy Hunter with this level of understanding!

She took a hanky from her pocket and blew her nose. Confessing Polly's crime had been a terrible thing to do, especially to someone like Jeremy Hunter, and she realised that she'd almost begun to sob. 'So…' She sniffed. 'Now that you know our…dark side, you'll be wanting to reconsider your proposition. We're in disgrace and I feel freaked out about it, to be truthful—even though I find it hard to blame my sister.'

Now he caught hold of her again, his voice raw. 'You idiot, Cryssie,' he said. 'Do you really think that my opinion of you is altered in any way by what you've just told me? For heaven's sake, give me some credit, woman!' He folded his arms around her, and despite her tortured emotions she found herself wallowing in the feel of him, of his arms wrapped around her. 'On the contrary, this makes my—ambitions— even more worthy of consideration, don't you agree?' he murmured. 'Just think. We can arrange the best possible treatment for Polly—which she is desperately in need of. And as for Milo.' He released her and turned away for a second. 'Nothing will be too good for Milo. He'll go to a top school, have whatever is needed to help him grow into a fully-rounded adult. And not totally influenced by over-protective women all the time.'

The tone of his voice was throbbing, urgent, and, despite being stung by some of his remarks, Cryssie felt herself beginning to let her mind think the unthinkable. Could she really go against all her preconceived notions and go along with his request? But what sort of a union would it be? she asked herself. He'd spelt out all the pros and cons in a way that only someone like Jed Hunter could—but, as always, it did make some sense! Could she honestly afford to turn him down? Yet what woman looked for a sensible marriage? Not that there wouldn't be moments of passion—he'd demonstrated that side of his nature before—but…love? He didn't know the meaning of the word. And what was the chilling phrase he'd used when describing his ex-marriage? That his 'terms and conditions' didn't tally? What on earth could *that* have meant?

Jed glanced at her, realising the thoughts which must be teeming through her mind. After all, what he'd just put to her had come as a complete shock—she had never had any designs on him, or his wealth, which was something he'd had to battle with from *other* females for most of his life. Thinking briefly of his ex-wife, he curled his lip dismissively. Ella and the woman standing so close to him were like chalk and cheese!

The afternoon started to slip by, and presently it seemed to Cryssie that this was just another meeting that he'd called. They sat apart, not touching now, and Jed broached one or two other topics relating to work—which calmed Cryssie down and made her feel less uneasy. But she knew that he would expect her to make a decision, and that he didn't like being kept waiting!

But he wasn't going to get her answer that quickly! He'd presented her with the biggest crisis she'd ever had to face, and she needed time to think it out. And who could she ask for advice? she thought miserably. Certainly not Polly. For the first time in a long while Cryssie felt lonely and insecure. The future which had seemed so straightforward now appeared fraught with impossible upheaval and drama. Jed Hunter's input had seen to that!

As if reading her thoughts, he said, 'I'm going to be out of the office tomorrow, and part of next week, so that'll give you some time to yourself—to make up your mind.' He smiled darkly at her troubled features. 'Just take a step back, Cryssie, and relax. Look at the whole picture. You'll begin to see that I'm right about this. About us.'

Of course Mr Always Right was never wrong, she thought, staring up at him, at the strong mouth and determined jaw. But if she did agree—and it was a big if—what would everyone think? And did that matter any more?

Suddenly he said cheerfully, 'I'm going to take you out for dinner tonight—we'll eat early so as not to be late getting back. Are you hungry?'

'No,' Cryssie replied promptly, completely robbed of any appetite.

'Well, that's too bad,' he said. 'Because after any important discussions I'm always starving!' He glanced at his watch. 'Go and tidy up, and I'll book a table somewhere rather special that I know.' When she didn't move, he pulled her roughly to her feet. 'Come on—I promise you that you won't be able to resist what's on offer. And it'll be a small celebration to mark the next important step which I hope you'll be taking!'

CHAPTER ELEVEN

THE following Wednesday evening, sitting in the room which he used as his office at Shepherd's Keep, Jed stared at his computer with blank eyes. The several meetings he'd attended over the previous few days had been productive enough, but throughout his time away from the area his main and overriding thought had been his proposal of marriage to Cryssie— and her refusal! That was not going to be the last word on the matter—even though he knew he had some way to go to make her see the validity of his plans. But…he'd succeed. Oh, yes, he'd succeed.

He got up and moved across to stare out of the window. The gardens looked equally lovely at night-time, he thought briefly, etched out as they were by beams from the spot lights. He knew Cryssie would love seeing it like this…her child-like reaction would be spontaneous. Here would be the perfect setting to make her change her mind, he mused.

His jaw clenched at his own situation—a situation he'd never imagined he'd find himself in. Trying to convince a female that he was good marriage material! Women had always found him attractive—he'd known that since his teens—and he'd enjoyed every minute of the attention he'd got. He was also aware that wealth—for which he had to thank his parents—was a powerful aphrodisiac. But the big downside was that those two advantages brought their own problems, and meeting so many members of the opposite sex had made him realise that it would never be easy to choose one woman whom he could trust—and tolerate—and who would be useful to him. And who didn't have her eye on the main chance. He admitted that he'd thought Ella would fit all his criteria when they'd first got together, but no one could have guessed how *that* would turn out!

He turned away, annoyed that his ex-wife had crept into his thoughts. It was Cryssie whom he had to win over, and getting to her through her family seemed the way to do it. Because he knew that they would always come first. He shrugged. He didn't care which route he used, just so long as he got there in the end.

His mobile rang suddenly, interrupting his reverie.

'Jed? I want to speak to you…I must speak to you…' Cryssie said, and hearing her voice made him smile.

'Of course… When?'

'Now—tonight. I need to speak to you…in private.' There was a pause. 'It's important.'

He grinned to himself. Of course it was!

'I'll pick you up in about forty minutes.' He hesitated, thinking quickly. 'There's a country pub I know. Where we won't be disturbed,' he added.

Cryssie's knees trembled as she put down the receiver. How was he going to take this! She knew very well that he didn't like having his plans overturned but—well, for once in his life he was going to have to accept it. And what about her? she asked herself, her shoulders drooping for a second. Was she really letting this opportunity slip away for ever? And—much,

much more vital—could she close the door on a relationship that she had never dreamed would ever come her way? Every time they had been close, and he had touched her, had left an indelible mark on her consciousness, her memory. She swallowed hard on the lump in her throat.

She made her excuses to Polly, who glanced at her anxiously.

'Are you going to see Jed?' she asked.

'Umm…yes, I think so,' Cryssie replied vaguely, hating the way she was always having to be evasive to Polly—and to everyone else. Well, that was all going to stop! If she could gather up all her strength to face her employer with the unpleasant facts, she might be able to return to the straightforward and uncomplicated life she'd lived before she'd met him.

Presently, as they drove into the countryside, he glanced across at her. 'I'm very flattered that you seem so anxious to see me, Cryssie,' he said. 'I hope you've been doing a lot of thinking!'

Cryssie closed her eyes for a minute, to stop the tears she felt from actually materialising. And why was she about to cry? she asked herself. Was it for Jed, or Milo, or Polly…or for herself? She was honest enough to admit that this time her tears were purely selfish.

Jed drew up outside a small pub almost at the end of a narrow country road. It was well-lit and inviting, and as he went in before her Cryssie wished that time would stop, and that there wouldn't be any need for her to inform him of the drastic step she was about to take. Not just because she knew he would be absolutely furious, but because she was practically being ripped to pieces by her divided loyalties. To her colleagues, to her family, but mostly to him!

He found a quiet corner table for them in the lounge bar, and looked down at her curiously as he pulled out a chair for her to sit down. 'Would you like a glass of champagne?' He smiled at her mischievously. 'I hope this is to be a celebration!'

She didn't look up. 'You choose,' she said dully, and he turned at once to go to the bar.

Presently he returned, with a glass of champagne for her and an orange juice for him. Cryssie immediately took a gulp of her drink before glancing up and looking at him for the first time. Those intense windows of his soul had their usual impact, and she blurted it out before losing her will-power. 'I cannot work for you, Jed. Nor marry you. I'm sorry. Something has happened which makes it impossible. It's over between us. Please don't say anything to make me change my mind. Please!'

Now the tears began to flow, and he let her weep silently for several seconds. 'You will give me the privilege of an explanation, I hope, Cryssie?' he said flatly.

Taking another clean tissue from her bag, she dabbed at her eyes and nose, realising that she must look a complete mess. She hadn't even put a comb through her hair since she'd come home from work. She looked up, her eyes red and swimming, and suddenly the words poured out while he listened.

'A few days ago,' she began, 'Dave and Joe—two of the senior members of staff—called us all together with a serious proposal. They want to start a co-operative and for us to continue trading under another name—"New Hydebound". Dave's got a relative who'll let us use a restored barn on his land where we can set everything up. There's good dry storage space for supplies, and a sort of office space for the computers.' She paused to drink some more wine before adding quickly, 'And they seem to have done their homework. They're getting a loan from the bank and putting up their houses as collateral.'

She paused, biting her lip until it hurt. 'And I'm forced to go with them—because it would be almost impossible without Rose and me. Between us we've always done the cataloguing, ordering, invoicing—all the technical stuff a newcomer would take months to grasp. And the accounts have always been my job.' She didn't dare look him in the eye. 'So how could I say, well, you all carry on, because I've got a super job lined up with the Hunter group—I don't need New Hydebound?' She shook her head helplessly. 'If I did that, the whole idea would almost certainly stall.' She gulped, closing her eyes briefly. 'As for your other…offer—well, that's irrelevant now, isn't it? I've simply got to throw my lot in with this idea, help to make it work.'

Jed gave a snort of angry derision. 'And what makes you think you can succeed where the Lewises so dismally failed?' he began.

'It'll take time,' she said quickly. 'But we've got a sound customer base, and everyone likes to support something new, support the underdog.' She looked away. 'I think it was when Frank, who's in charge of stock control, shed tears because all is not lost after all that my mind was made up.'

'Very touching,' Jed remarked dryly.

'I will return all the money you've already paid me as soon as I can,' she said, swallowing hard as she spoke, and wondering when she was going to be able to do that!

'And what are you all going to live on until these big orders start rolling in?' he asked sarcastically.

'Well, the final bonuses you're paying will be sufficient for the time being,' she began, 'and—'

'Hmm. Perhaps I shouldn't have been so hasty or so generous,' he said, and Cryssie looked up at him sharply.

'You did promise…'

'Of course,' he agreed curtly.

'I just cannot deny them this chance,' she said miserably. 'I can't let everyone down.'

'You're not so worried about letting *me* down!'

'I am worried!' Cryssie protested, the tears threatening again.

'And apparently not too upset about Milo and Polly's prospects either, are you?' he began, and she flared up at his words.

'Don't you dare keep bringing them into this,' she said, so fiercely that one or two other drinkers looked up in surprise. 'Anyway, somehow or other I'll make sure we have enough to get by!' She drained her glass. 'I've never had to rely on anyone before. And as for you, Jed, and *your* needs—losing my services isn't the end of the world. You'll find someone else to do exactly as you want.'

'I don't want someone else. I want you,' he said slowly. 'And I can't believe your lack of logic, Cryssie. Go on—admit it. You know very well what's best—the step you should really be taking—yet you persist in clinging to your over-developed sense of loyalty to an out-dated organisation that'll be wallowing in debt again before you know it!'

Cryssie stood up, knowing that this wasn't going anywhere and that there was nothing more to say. She knew he was furious and upset, and she couldn't really blame him—because she'd well and truly scuppered his plans on all fronts! And Jeremy Hunter did not like that!

They drove home and he stopped outside her door, switching off the engine. She knew that he was angry with her, and that anger seared her flesh with a burning heat. What she most wanted in all the world was for him to hold her, to comfort her, to tell her that he understood the problem and that somehow it would all come right. But he didn't do any of those things, only waited for her to get out of the car and leave. And, with the tears starting again, that was what she did. And this time he didn't even bother to get out and open the door for her.

In the house, Cryssie sank down onto the sofa and buried her face in her hands. What had she ever done to deserve all this trauma? she asked herself.

A light hand on her shoulder brought Cryssie back down to earth, and she looked up quickly to see Polly standing there in her nightdress.

'Cryss—whatever is the matter?' she asked gently, and for the first time in her memory Cryssie found herself in the unusual position of being comforted by her younger sister.

'I haven't bothered to tell you this before, Poll, but Jeremy Hunter is dismantling Hydebound in favour of a new hotel he wants to build on the site.' She blew her nose for the hundredth time. 'But the even more worrying thing is that the staff intend going it alone somewhere else. And I honestly don't know if it can work. But I must agree to go with them, even though Jed has offered me another position with him. But I can't take that, can I? I can't let the others down!'

'Of course you can, Cryssie!' Polly said. 'Leave them all to it and look out for yourself. If you've got the chance of something else you should grab it with both hands!' The girl's brow furrowed at the thought that their income might suddenly be threatened.

'No, I can't be the only one to throw cold water on the idea. It could be a last-ditch stand for some of them.' Cryssie got up. 'I must go to bed now—even if I don't manage to sleep. And don't worry, Poll. I'll make sure we don't starve!'

As he drove back to Shepherd's Keep, Jeremy Hunter's expression was dark. So, Crystal Rowe was quite prepared to ignore his requirements and her family's needs—plus the

offer of a gilt-edged future—in favour of a daft lame-duck
notion in order to satisfy her over-heightened sense of doing
the right thing! By everyone but him! His eyes narrowed as
he sped along the almost deserted roads. Whatever she said,
he was determined to have her—on his own terms. But she
was just as determined. He knew that. He and she were a
pigeon pair, he thought grimly.

Then a slow smile spread across his masterful features,
which were strongly outlined in the reflective light from the
powerful instrument panel in front of him. All right then, he
thought, with more than a hint of satisfaction. He had no intention of being thwarted at this stage of his life by a mere
slip of a girl who didn't know what was good for her! Arriving
home, he accelerated into the drive and crunched to a stop in
front of the big oak doors. There were winners and losers in
any skirmish, he thought, and he'd make damned sure which
one he'd be! Whatever it took!

CHAPTER TWELVE

THE next day, the atmosphere at Hydebound was charged with a tangible electricity as realisation of the step they were taking dawned. The employees' plan for the firm was still very new, but already everyone was imagining how it would get started, and whether the transition would prove more difficult than they expected. Although the concept was generally approved of, there was an undeniable anxiety underlying the optimism. What if it all went wrong? Were they up to the mammoth task of going it alone? And what would be the reaction from Jeremy Hunter when he heard about it? Not that it would be any of his business now, everyone argued.

Cryssie kept her head down during all the discussions, offering only vague comments, but knowing very well that when Jed put in an appearance she was going to have great difficulty in not betraying her feelings. She was now exactly where she had been on New Year's Eve, when he'd first arrived on the scene, she thought dully, with all her emotions at basement level. She was just another member of staff, with no special privileges, no expectations—and no pressures. But how could she pretend that everything that had happened between her and the man was nothing—of no importance? It had been the most highly coloured episode of her entire life—

dazzlingly, blindingly, so! And its impact had left her feeling as if she had been put through a mangle.

That Friday Cryssie was alone, sitting at her desk sifting through some of the final invoices, when her internal phone rang.

'Come into my office, please.' Jed's curt voice sent her heart straight into her mouth. She hadn't even realised he'd arrived! His interest in the place had seemed to be getting less and less as the end was approaching.

'Do you want to see any…files…records…?' she asked, trying not to let her voice sound as pathetic and little-girly as it seemed to her.

'No. No…thank you.'

Cryssie made a face to herself. He was in masterful mode!

She entered his office without knocking, and he got up from his chair to face her. His hair was in need of a trim, she thought involuntarily, with long boyish fronds curling into the nape of his neck below his crisp white collar. But he looked even more fatally handsome than ever, and Cryssie had to look away quickly. Could it only have been two days ago that they'd sat together in the pub while she'd given him the decision he hadn't wanted to hear? It seemed more like two years!

Now, she gazed at him steadily, and his own expression was equally determined. He didn't ask her to sit down.

'I've got some important news I think may interest you,' he said, coming straight to the point as usual, and Cryssie's mouth went dry. What was coming *this* time?

'I thought you ought to know that we intend converting part of the fourth floor of Latimer's to accommodate Hydebound, so that it can continue trading,' he announced. He was in Managing Director mode, not expecting any interruption— and he didn't get any because Cryssie was dumbstruck! 'It's actually been under review by the family before,' he went on, 'but we've now come to the conclusion that it would probably do very well. Initial costs will be absorbed by the rest of the store, and your loyal customers will soon get used to coming into town to buy their specialist leatherwork.'

If he'd just said that he was taking the whole place, lock, stock and barrel, on a trip to the moon, the effect could not have been more dramatic. Cryssie was almost knocked sideways.

'Naturally,' Jed said smoothly, 'I'm calling everyone in this afternoon to let them know, and to find out whether anyone wants to resign. And, more importantly, to know who's coming with us.' He paused, his eyes glinting with satisfaction at the effect his bombshell had had on Cryssie. 'And of course I expect…I'm anticipating…your opinion on the matter.'

For a few moments they stared at each other in complete silence. Then he quirked one eyebrow, his firm mouth betraying the merest hint of amusement, and it made Cryssie fume inwardly.

'Well? Are *you* in favour of the transfer, Crystal?'

She waited a few seconds before saying bluntly, 'I shall never forgive you.'

He raised both hands in mock surprise. 'Why? What is there to forgive? Aren't I doing exactly what you—of all people—wanted?'

'How could you do that to me? I still can't believe it!' she said angrily, colour rising in her cheeks. 'You said that you and the family have been considering this… Why, then, didn't you *tell* me the other night? Didn't you think I'd be *interested?*'

He came from behind the desk towards her, and she automatically backed away defensively. Suddenly she realised that she didn't want to trust this man any more—anything he said or did, anything about him. He was unknowable!

'Look, I've explained that moving Hydebound over to Latimer's is something the family have discussed before,' he said slowly, 'but we talked it over again yesterday, and we're in favour of giving it a go.' He paused. 'And I'm willing to bet that Hydebound stands a better chance of survival under the Latimer's roof than by giving it a new name and sticking it in a field somewhere. Impressed though I was at the courageous notion,' he added briefly.

By this time Cryssie's heart rate had begun to quieten, and she took a long, deep breath. What was this man *like?* She leant against a chair for a moment. 'And I take it that my own position is—' she began. He interrupted.

'Exactly the same as before. You are employed by the Hunter group, and whether you actually sit in the office at Latimer's, or come with me elsewhere is neither here nor there. For the moment. And it's no one else's business, either.' He smiled down at her darkly. 'It'll be easy for you now, Cryssie. No eyebrows will be raised when we're together. They'll all have what they want—their future security—and I'll have what I want.' He paused for a second. 'I'll have you.'

Suddenly the simple truth hit Cryssie with such unbelievable force that she nearly fainted. *Surely,* she thought, Jeremy Hunter would not go to such lengths just to get his own way in the matter of acquiring the assistant he wanted! The idea was so preposterous that she almost laughed out loud—a hysterical giggle that she knew wouldn't stop if she allowed it to start! The man was a monster if that was the case! It *couldn't* be that important to him, she thought. Even if the Hydebound staff *were* equal beneficiaries of his determination. But she was beginning to know Mr Jeremy Hunter, and the way his mind ticked! She felt sure her intuition was correct. Nothing would stand in the way of his wishes—whatever it took!

'I just don't *believe* you, Jed,' she said slowly. 'I don't believe you could have come to such an important decision virtually overnight.'

He shrugged, and now he put a hand on her arm, making her flinch. 'Believe what you like, Cryssie,' he said quietly. 'But before my hotel is up and running Hydebound will have recommenced operations under the Latimer's banner.' He treated her to another of his devastating slow smiles. 'A good result all round—wouldn't you agree?'

Of course! It was just that—a good result, business as usual, ends neatly tied, Cryssie thought. She should have been feeling over the moon at the news, but she didn't. She felt wary and disturbed, her mind a kaleidoscope of shifting patterns. There was so much she liked about Jeremy Hunter, but his self-centred, thrusting determination to get exactly what he wanted at all times could be a distinctly unpleasant character-istic—and one which she'd seen enough of to last a lifetime! But then she remembered how wonderful he'd been with Milo at Shepherd's Keep, so obviously enjoying the little boy's company. He'd changed from a hard-nosed business execu-tive into a totally relaxed individual, reliving his own child-hood. And what about everything else? When they'd touched, when he'd held her… She shivered visibly as her mind ran on like a runaway train.

Afterwards, she couldn't remember how long they must have stood there in complete silence, but finally as she turned to leave the room, he said, 'We have plenty of things to discuss, Cryssie. I'm sure you will agree that there are some impor-tant details still to be sorted and, since there's no time like the present, perhaps you'd allow me to buy you dinner tonight?'

'No—I'm sorry…I'm not free tonight,' Cryssie said firmly. 'Some other time.' The only thing she wanted to do was to stay at home, shut the doors and hide under the bed! she thought. The thought of spending about four hours in close proximity to Jeremy Hunter discussing 'important' details was the most unattractive prospect she could envisage!

'Tomorrow night, then,' he said. 'I'll book a table at the Laurels—you enjoyed it last time, didn't you?'

Later that evening, after she'd put Milo to bed, Cryssie sat down opposite Polly, who was idly flicking through a magazine. Glancing at her sister, Cryssie envied her the ability she seemed to have of switching off her troubles—she'd not referred to the matter of the stolen scarf since the evening she'd poured out her heart to Cryssie, though each time Jed's name came up her features did express a fleeting anxiety. But that was just like Polly, Cryssie thought, she always did brush any fears under the carpet, out of sight, hoping they'd go away—or hoping that Cryssie would *make* them go away.

But the one that didn't go away was fast asleep upstairs, and Cryssie smiled to herself. Sometimes a nightmare could turn into the sweetest of dreams, she thought. Then her brow furrowed. She herself had been living between those two scenarios ever since Jed Hunter had entered her life—and it wasn't over yet! Yes, she still had her job—and, yes, all her colleagues and friends at Hydebound had theirs. The reaction to the news that afternoon, when Jed had explained what he intended doing, had been one hundred per cent in favour. The relief had naturally been spontaneous and genuine, and Cryssie had joined in with the general surprise and gratitude, being careful not to look at Jed, because she'd known what she'd see in those penetrating black eyes. Total smug satisfaction! But in spite of all the positives, the mountain she still had to climb was her decision about his proposal of marriage.

That was something that would not go away—not something that could be brushed under the carpet—because she knew he wouldn't give up until he'd beaten her into submission. The thought made her want to scream, because it went against all her natural instincts of survival. And it was a quandary she'd never had to face before.

'I had an important meeting with Jed today,' Cryssie said now, and Polly looked up from what she was reading. 'Hydebound is going to re-open at Latimer's,' Cryssie said briefly, 'so the other idea I told you about is out of the window. It's not going to happen.'

'Well, that's a relief all round, isn't it?' Polly faltered, her colour rising at the mere name of the shop, which she'd kept well clear of lately. 'So we won't have to worry about money, will we, Cryssie? I mean, if things hadn't worked out we could have ended up penniless!'

Money. That was the bottom line in Polly's book, Cryssie thought. And in someone else's she could mention! Well, somehow she was going to have to keep her job and keep him at bay at the same time. Because she was more convinced than ever that she could not marry a man who was so obsessed with getting his own way that he would allow nothing to obstruct his plans.

Much later, after Polly had gone to bed, the phone rang and Cryssie's heart leapt. That had to be Jed—no one else would ring at this hour!

'Cryssie? I'm at the General Hospital…'

'Why…? What is it…? Are you hurt…?' Her mouth went dry. He'd had an accident! 'Are you…all right…?'

'Yes, yes, it's okay—I'm all right. It's my father…he's had a heart attack.' There was a pause. 'He's in a pretty bad way, I'm afraid…'

'Oh, Jed! I'm *so* sorry!' Cryssie's mind immediately conjured up a vision of that handsome silver-haired man lying helpless in a hospital bed. 'What…when did this happen?'

'A couple of hours ago. I was working in the office at Shepherd's Keep—my mother is away staying with friends—and I heard a crash. He'd collapsed in the hallway. The ambulance came pretty quickly, but—'

'I'm coming over,' Cryssie said at once. 'It'll take me about forty-five minutes from here.'

'Oh…are you sure, Cryssie… Would you mind? It's late.'

'I'm coming over.'

Driving as fast as her ancient car would allow, Cryssie made for the local General Hospital, feeling as anxious and fearful as if this was someone of her own. Henry was a big, powerful man… Who could begin to imagine those black, twinkling eyes closed perhaps for ever? And Jed's voice on the phone… Strong as ever, but tonight it had seemed different. He clearly wanted someone there with him. Alice was obviously too far away to get there quickly—so he'd rung Cryssie! A surprising warmth ran through her body as she thought about it. At this moment Jeremy Hunter's need had nothing to do with business, or profit and loss. What he was experiencing now was a natural human desire to be close to someone he trusted, who could support him as he watched his father lie seriously ill.

By the time she arrived Henry had been moved into a small side ward where Jed was standing, staring out of the window. He turned quickly to see her. And, without the slightest thought that it wasn't the thing to do, Cryssie ran across and put her arms around his waist, holding him so tightly they could have been one person. And he didn't let her go as she buried her face in his neck, a tiny sob escaping her lips.

It didn't take much for her to remember those other times she'd visited hospitals…holding Great-Aunt Josie's hand as she and Polly had whispered goodbye to their parents, losing their battle to live after the accident, and then seeing Josie, who'd been so strong for them, lying inert after a fatal stroke. She and Polly had had each other to cling to then—but who did Jed have at this precise moment? No one, she thought fleetingly. He'd had to ring his PA to support him in this very human moment.

Eventually she slid away from his embrace, and together they went across to the bed where Henry lay quite still, being kept alive by wires and bubbling sachets of liquid. Still holding his hand, Cryssie looked up into Jed's troubled face. The strong features had suddenly taken on a haggard look, she thought, and dark stubble was already forming on the line of his jaw.

'What do they say, Jed? What have they told you?' she whispered.

'Not much,' he replied quietly. 'The next forty-eight hours are crucial, apparently. My mother is in Edinburgh, so there's no way she can get here at this time of night. I've made arrangements for a flight for her in the morning—she'll know about it at first light—and I've ordered a car ready to pick her up at the airport and bring her straight here. I've left messages with her hosts.' He looked away for a second. 'I…apologise…for ringing you, Cryssie,' he said. 'But I didn't—'

'You don't need to apologise,' Cryssie said quickly. 'I'm glad…I'm pleased you felt you could,' she added softly.

He gazed down at her then, for a long moment, and his eyes seemed to melt into pools of melted dark chocolate…soft, liquid, and appealing. He was appealing for warmth, compassion and understanding. And in Cryssie he'd come to the right person!

The sister came in then, to check on her patient, and she

smiled at Cryssie, who was still standing close to the bed, holding Jed's hand. She took in the girl's appearance at a glance, taking pity on the frail figure, pale face and anxious green eyes. 'Try not to worry too much, Mrs Hunter,' the woman said kindly. 'Your father-in-law is in good hands.' She paused. 'Would you like some tea—or coffee? I'll get a nurse to bring you some.'

'A cup of tea would be lovely,' Cryssie said—almost adding, 'And my husband would like black coffee.' But she stopped herself in time! The sister had clearly put two and two together and come up with five. But somehow it hadn't come as the nasty shock Cryssie might have expected!

'Black coffee, please,' Jed said, and the moment passed— but not before he'd caught her eye and winked, just slightly. Perhaps he hoped that the natural mistake the woman had made would set the seal on his requirements? Cryssie thought. But now was not the time to go into all that. This present trauma was a matter of life and death—and there wasn't anything that her control freak of a boss could do about either.

Their drinks arrived, and they sat down on two hard-backed chairs.

'I can't really believe this is happening.' Jed shook his head. 'My father has been so well. He's obviously on medication all the time, but this is totally unexpected…'

'No one ever expects the worst to happen,' Cryssie said slowly. 'And when it does we're never prepared for it. How could we be? We're not gods…none of us…we're just poor human beings, trying to make the best of everything, of every day. Whatever it may bring.'

Jed looked at her as if seeing her properly for the first time. Why was it that he didn't want to take his eyes off the woman? he asked himself. As usual, there was nothing special about her appearance—she was dressed anonymously, as she normally was, her hair hanging loose around her face. Yet there was this thing about her…her simplicity, her vulnerability, her amazing stoicism and bravery. Suddenly he began to feel ashamed at the deck of cards that fate had handed *him*.

They drank in silence for a few moments, and, glancing across at him, Cryssie had an almost insane desire to clutch him to her and smother his face with kisses—as she did when Milo had fallen down and hurt himself. She wanted to tell Jed that it would be okay…that it would be better tomorrow… And those sudden thoughts shocked her momentarily. Had Jed been right when he'd accused her of only wanting to nurture everyone, to look after people? *Was* that what her instincts were really all about? But then she remembered how she'd felt when he'd enveloped her in an almost overpowering embrace! *That* had been her need for passionate loving from the most achingly handsome man she was ever likely to meet!

She looked up and saw him staring at her.

'Come back from wherever you are,' he said. 'You were miles away. What are you thinking?'

Their eyes met in a long, lingering gaze, and for a while neither spoke, both lost in the private world of their own thoughts. A pretty blush rose in Cryssie's cheeks at what *she'd* been dwelling on a few seconds before! Imagine if she said, Well, Jed, I was actually thinking how good it would feel if you were to make love to me!

'I wasn't really thinking about anything,' she lied. 'Only that time seems to stand still in these places.'

And as for Jed, his own interpretation of what had been going on behind her captivating green eyes was that she probably wished she was safely home in bed, listening out for Milo. Yet he knew that wasn't true. She'd insisted on being here with him. And there was no one in the world he'd rather have near him than this unlikely woman who seemed to have invaded every part of his consciousness since the day they'd met.

The minutes ticked by, with various comings and goings from the staff, and presently Jed said, 'You must be worn out, Cryssie. But I don't want you to go home yet…I mean, not now, in the middle of the night. Can you stay another couple of hours—until daylight? I'd feel happier you driving home then.'

'Of course I can stay,' Cryssie said at once. 'And I don't feel tired. I seldom do in emergencies.'

Jed nodded, pleased. Going out into the main ward, he brought back two soft chairs and put them together. 'Here— no one's going to need these until tomorrow,' he said. 'At least you can lie down for a bit. There's even two cushions.'

Obediently Cryssie lay down, as instructed, and had to admit that it felt good to rest her back. It had been another long, long day, and in the silence of the room her eyes began to droop and her mind drifted briefly into a semi-doze.

Sitting there, Jed swept his gaze from his elderly father to the woman who hadn't hesitated to drive a distance at night to be at his side His eyes softened as he watched her breathing gently, with one small hand tucked beneath her chin.

And, even in his present anxiety and concern, his overriding thought was that he was now more determined than ever that Cryssie should never escape his plan—for both their futures!

CHAPTER THIRTEEN

DURING the following days there was obviously a lot of discussion going on at Hydebound, as to whether the move to Latimer's would now take place, given the traumatic time the Hunter family was going through. But one day Jed came into the office, unsmiling and businesslike as usual, to assure everyone that nothing had changed.

He was away a lot of the time after that, and Cryssie was glad of the respite it gave her—from seeing him, from thinking of how she was going to be strong enough to withstand his persistence. Because she knew he was not going to give up. Part of her so badly wanted to accept his proposal of marriage—yet there was a more than niggling doubt that she'd be doing the right thing. Her past would keep rearing its ugly head, filling her with misgivings, and Jed's obvious motives just did not fit in with her own ideas of what made a successful marriage—one that would stand the test of time.

He had rung her several times with progress reports on his father's condition, and for a long time it didn't look good for Henry. Jed and Alice spent most of this time at his bedside, and Cryssie wished with all her heart that she could do something to help. But what *could* she do that they couldn't afford to pay for? she asked herself.

One thing they could not buy was the 'Get Well' card which Milo made for the invalid. It showed a picture of a house with smoke coming from the chimney, and a garden with flowers, and two matchstick people playing football. And right around the four sides the little boy had added brightly coloured kisses, with the words 'With love from Milo' in his own childish writing added at the end.

Jed rang specially to speak to Milo, and the two held a long and serious conversation which Cryssie could only half-hear as she listened. But Milo's face was wreathed in smiles as he heard what Jed was saying.

'Well, what was all that about?' she asked.

'Not telling. It's a secret,' the child replied, running off.

Eventually, the call Cryssie most wanted to hear came, on a Saturday morning just as she was filling the machine with all their week's washing.

'Hi, Cryssie…I thought you'd like to know that my father came out of hospital yesterday, and—'

'Oh, Jed! That's terrific news! You said last week that they were a lot more optimistic. This is *so* good to hear!'

'Yes, I think we're out of the woods at last,' Jed said. 'But I'm afraid I do have a request. Henry wants to see you—he'd love you to come over, if you could spare us a couple of hours.'

'Of course I can!' Cryssie said at once. 'When were you thinking of?'

'Now—today—if possible. I know it's your day for doing things, and taking Milo somewhere, but—'

'That doesn't matter—it's okay,' Cryssie said, thinking that those were trivial considerations compared with spending a short time with someone who had so recently cheated death. 'I could leave in about half an hour or so—and I won't stay long, because I don't want to tire Henry out. I'm sure he'll need a lot of rest for a while.'

'I could come over and fetch you—' Jed began, but she interrupted.

'No—no, there's no need. I know exactly how to get to you, and it would be silly, you having to make four trips.' If she drove herself, it also meant that she could leave when she wanted to, Cryssie thought. Without waiting for Jed to make up his mind about when he would bring her back.

'It'll be good to see you, Cryssie,' Jed said slowly. 'I've missed you,' he added. 'And I've actually missed going to work each day. I've decided that I don't much care for illness and hospitals.'

'I've never met anyone yet who does,' Cryssie replied dryly. 'But you were right to stay there, with Alice and Henry. We must all be aware of where our priorities lie.'

They rang off just as Polly and Milo came downstairs, and Cryssie told them where she was going.

'Can I come too, Cryssie?' Milo asked eagerly.

'Oh—don't you want to go to the park after all, darling?' Polly asked hopefully.

'No. I want to go to Jed's house. Please, Cryssie…can I?'

Cryssie poured some cereal into a dish for the little boy, and he clambered up into his seat at the kitchen table. 'I'm sorry, sweetheart. You know that Jed's father has been very ill, don't you? You made him that lovely card, didn't you? Well, he's getting better, but he has to keep very quiet for a little while, so not many visitors are allowed, I'm afraid.'

'But I wouldn't make a noise,' Milo persisted, picking up his spoon.

'No, I know you wouldn't,' Cryssie said gently. 'But, look, if you go with Mummy to the park this morning, I promise that I'll take you to Jed's house soon.' Cryssie paused, wondering when that might be. 'And I shan't be late back. We'll do something special then, okay?'

'What like?' Milo said grumpily.

'The summer fair has come to town. We could go for an hour this evening.'

'Yeah!' Milo cried, cheering up a lot.

Presently she got dressed and went downstairs. Polly glanced at her. 'Mmm, you look nice, Cryssie,' she said, noting her sister's simple white cotton blouse, and the short denim skirt which emphasised her slim legs. 'And I like your hair done like that.'

'Like what?' Cryssie asked, knowing very well that she had taken more trouble with it than usual.

'I like the knot really high on your head, with the curly strands escaping around your face…it suits you.'

'Oh—thanks,' Cryssie said, looking away. She *had* arranged it differently today, she admitted—but why? She knew the answer to that! Why was she having this tug of war with herself? she agonised silently. I want him to want me; I don't want him to want me; I don't want to want *him!*

It was almost lunchtime when she made her way slowly up the long drive at Shepherd's Keep. It was a perfect June day, and the spring flowers she'd admired last time had been taken over by ranks of bright red tulips. Cryssie sighed. This place was like a little bit of heaven, she thought.

Seeing that another car had already been parked in front of the big wooden entrance door, she stopped a little way away, and got out just as Jed came across the garden to meet her. He looked lean and suave, dressed in chinos and an open-neck black shirt. Realising that this was the first time they'd come face to face, alone, since the night they'd been at the hospital made an unusual shyness sweep over Cryssie. She was totally confused about her true position in life, she told herself. Confused about almost everything!

But Jed was as self-possessed as ever, and he bent and claimed her lips as if it was the norm. How far they'd come, she thought. But…how? Helplessly, she didn't resist, but closed her eyes in a kind of wonder that this man should play such havoc with her life, with her emotions. One moment she was sure that she could never trust him, the next she was certain that he was all she wanted!

Their kiss was not a perfunctory fusing of two pairs of lips, but a lingering moment of noon-day passion—sweeter, somehow, in the warm daylight than on other more obviously romantic occasions. He paused, looking down into her upturned face, then kissed her again, a little more urgently this time. After a moment she pulled away breathlessly. 'I've actually come to see Henry,' she reminded him, and he took her by the hand.

'And so you shall—but the doctor arrived a few minutes before you, so we'll go over to the lodge for a bit, until he's gone.'

Hand in hand, they strolled over the lush green grass, and Cryssie felt a pang of guilt. Milo would love to be here now, she thought. He would just race around the acres of space, as free as a bird. Instead of that he was having to make do with the rather scruffy little local park. She shrugged inwardly. She'd make it up to him, she thought.

They got to the lodge and went inside, and Jed pulled Cryssie down beside him on the swing chair.

'A lot seems to have happened since we were here last,' Cryssie said, trying to stem the tide of anxiety that was rising inside her. This was the perfect place, and time, for Jed to try and pin her down—to force her to change her mind about not accepting his proposal of marriage. And, if he did, was she ready with her answer?

'Yes, a lot *has* happened,' he agreed. 'For both of us.'

'I seem to remember that we were discussing business last time,' Cryssie said. 'Talking of which—what about the trouble at your hotel in Wales?'

'Oh—with everything else that's been going on I forgot to tell you,' Jed replied. 'It sorted itself out in the end, would you believe? Max's wife is pregnant—don't ask me who the father is, because I don't care! And Max and his wife are over the moon—they've wanted children for ages. So she's given in her notice, and Kevin will have to look elsewhere for his entertainment.' He smiled down at Cryssie. 'But it was so good that you were the one who rumbled the whole sorry mess, and so good to have you to talk to about it, too, Cryssie. It cleared my mind. So... thanks.'

Cryssie smiled back, genuinely pleased that that particular thorn had been removed.

Jed leaned back for a second, his hands behind his head. 'I'm afraid all business topics have taken rather a back seat lately,' he admitted. 'But I'll be in harness again next week. Luckily for me, all our management personnel are more than reliable, and can be trusted to act on their own initiative when necessary. They've all been very sympathetic with the present situation, and nothing's ground to a halt—so far as I know.'

Cryssie stared at him thoughtfully. Although he seemed to have a reputation for being cold and hard sometimes, he paid well, and was generally admired and respected. She could imagine that all his staff would do their utmost to keep everything running smoothly.

They were silent for several moments, before he slowly

turned to her, putting his arm across her shoulders, tucking her in towards him. 'What do I have to do to convince you what your next vital step should be, Cryssie?' he murmured. 'You must have been giving it some thought. Haven't events helped you come to your decision?' As if to add a further dimension to his question, he cupped her face in his hands and kissed her—very gently, but with an added sense of purpose.

Luckily Cryssie was spared having to say anything in reply, as at that moment Alice's voice could be heard calling. Sighing, Jed released her, and they both stood up as the woman came in.

'Ah, there you are!' Alice said. 'I thought this was where I'd find you! The doctor's just gone, and Henry is about to have a little sleep, but he insists on seeing Cryssie first.' She gave the girl a hug, and Cryssie responded warmly.

'Alice—I can't tell you how worried we've all been. And we're so thankful that Henry is on the road to recovery.'

'Thank you, my dear. But he's got strict instructions to take it easy…with only a very occasional glass of champagne to cheer him up!'

Together, the three went into the house. Upstairs, Henry was lying propped up in bed, with massive pillows behind his head. On the small table by his side Cryssie couldn't help noticing Milo's card, already displayed, and, following her gaze, Henry pointed his finger. 'That was the thing that helped me get better,' he said, smiling. 'And I want to thank Milo in person soon.'

'I'll arrange it—don't worry,' Jed promised.

They stayed for less than half an hour before Cryssie realised that the older man was looking weary. 'I must go home now, Henry,' she said gently. 'But when you're stronger I'll come to see you again.'

Downstairs, Megan had already gone home for the afternoon, but on the kitchen table she'd left a beautifully prepared cold luncheon, and without much persuading Cryssie sat down and helped herself to fresh bread, salad and cheese. Sitting next to her, Jed poured her a glass of water.

'Not quite the dinner date we were going to have at the Laurels, is it?' he murmured. 'But that one's on ice for another time.'

Cryssie broke off a piece of bread and buttered it. 'This'll do me nicely for now.' She smiled.

Presently, they walked slowly back to her car, neither wanting to bring this part of the day to an end.

'Henry has really been through the mill, hasn't he?' Cryssie said. 'He still looks strong enough, but his eyes say it all.'

'Well, he'll only ever be as strong as his heart is,' Jed said slowly. 'My parents are actually talking about going to live abroad somewhere, where it's warmer. Well, my mother is, and she'll persuade my father eventually. Spain, probably, or the South of France, where they can spend at least the cold months of the English winter.'

'That sounds a very good idea,' Cryssie said.

'Yes, but of course at first my father thought he couldn't possibly be so far away from the business. I told him that was ridiculous. Communications mean that we can be in constant touch, and if necessary we can be together in a matter of a couple of hours or so. Travel's no problem. Not today.' He paused. 'And, as my mother has pointed out, now that *you're* part of our set-up, they know that I'll have all the support I need.'

Cryssie looked at him sharply. Was this another tactic to make her see things his way? Another piece of emotional blackmail? she thought.

'But…Shepherd's Keep will feel very empty with just me rattling around in it,' he ventured, and Cryssie sighed inwardly.

She knew exactly what was behind *that* remark! Yet somehow it didn't upset her. What he'd said was a fact, whether he'd meant to add it to his weaponry of persuasion or not. Giving him a sidelong glance, she thought it was hard to think of him living alone in the vast house, with only the elderly Megan to keep some semblance of order and prepare his meals. She didn't think his culinary skills were up to much, considering the remark he'd made at his London flat about the two omelettes he'd managed to produce.

They reached her car, and reluctantly Jed opened the door for Cryssie to get in—just as her mobile rang.

'That has to be Polly,' Cryssie said, frowning. 'Wonder what she wants—she seldom rings me.' As she answered it, her face immediately creased in anxiety. 'What? When, Polly? What do you mean?'

Witnessing her consternation, Jed automatically gripped Cryssie's hand, putting his arm around her to support her.

'Tell me again. What time?' Cryssie's voice rose to a shrill pitch. 'How long?'

Jed's brow furrowed. This was obviously a frantic message. Then, 'Call the police now…*now*, Poll! And don't leave the house! Stay where you are!' She looked up at Jed, and he'd never seen her face so contorted in such anguish. He raised his eyebrows questioningly, but Polly was obviously going on talking as Cryssie listened. 'I'll be home soon, Polly. Keep calm, Polly. Stop it! Listen to me! Get the police—and *stay* there!' Cryssie almost shouted.

She rang off, and stared up at Jed as if the end of the world was happening right then.

'What the *hell* is it?' he demanded.

'It's Milo. He's gone…he's missing. Polly can't find him anywhere!' Then she gathered herself together. 'I've got to go…I've got to get home now!'

Jed slammed the door shut and grabbed her arm. 'We'll take my car,' he said. 'Come on—we'll get there in half the time!'

CHAPTER FOURTEEN

SICK with apprehension, Cryssie sat stiffly alongside Jed as, tight-lipped, he drove rapidly away from Shepherd's Keep. They hardly exchanged a word for several minutes. She was so white with fear that at one point she thought she was going to faint—something he was obviously aware of, because, glancing across at her, he muttered tersely, 'Put your head between your knees, Cryssie! And get a grip—we'll be there soon!'

A police car was already outside the house, and Jed drew up swiftly behind it. Hardly waiting for him to stop, Cryssie flung open the door and ran up the path. Inside, a police-woman was sitting by Polly on the settee, taking notes, while another officer stood turning the pages of the latest album of photographs of Milo, asking questions soothingly.

As soon as she saw Cryssie, Polly jumped to her feet and flung her arms around her, bursting into hysterical tears. 'Cryssie! I'm so sorry! Milo's never run off before, has he? He was always so safe in the garden! Whatever shall we do? Oh, Cryssie…this is a nightmare! I've looked everywhere!'

Jed introduced himself briefly to the officers, and in answer to his questions they explained that all the area cars were already patrolling the streets, that missing children were a number one priority, and that in most cases they turned up safe and sound.

For a child of five to be missing for three hours was not uncommon.

'They're usually with someone they know,' the man said reassuringly, trying to make himself heard above Polly's wailing. 'The best thing is for his mother—and his aunt—to stay here, for when he wanders back home. The WPC will stay too—and I'll go to cover one of the possible areas where the child might be.' He glanced down at one of the pictures he was holding. 'He's a beautiful little boy,' he said casually—which only added to Polly's hysteria.

'Cryssie—you come with me,' Jed said brusquely, and through her threatening tears she could see clearly that he was agonising over this situation as much as herself and Polly. 'You know all the places he goes—all his friends,' he added.

'But I've been everywhere. I've already done that!' Polly cried.

'Then we'll do it all again,' Jed said firmly. 'Maybe there's somewhere you've overlooked.' He grabbed Cryssie's hand. 'Come on. We're wasting time!'

The rest of the afternoon passed in a haze of hope and despair as one by one all possible ideas of where Milo might be came to nothing. The minutes ticked by as they drove slowly along every road, searching the park and the surrounding small wooded area where the children made dens, questioning everyone they came across, holding up Milo's picture, until Cryssie felt so physically and mentally drained she thought she was going to lose her mind. It was obvious that the police had not been successful, either. Because they'd promised to ring Jed's mobile if the child turned up.

Feeling defeat begin to sweep over her, she turned to Jed and said helplessly, 'He's gone, Jed. He's been stolen. I know it. We're never going to see him again.'

'*No!*' He snarled out the word in a way that made Cryssie recoil in fear. 'No, *no!* We've *got* to find him! Come on… think!' He banged his fist against his forehead in frustration. 'What about…didn't you say you were taking him to the Summer Fair at some point? He might have tried to make his own way—'

'That's impossible,' Cryssie said at once. 'He'd never do that! It's right at the other side of town—there's no way he could get there by himself.'

Jed revved the engine. 'It's worth a try,' he said tersely.

They drove through the crowded Saturday afternoon streets without speaking. Jed's face was almost brutal in expression as he surged the car forward. Cryssie sat motionless, listening to the racing of her heart. If anything dreadful had happened to Milo—or worse, if she should never see him again—her life would be over, she thought. Because what would there be to live for? All her plans and hopes and dreams were wrapped up in that little boy, and for Polly it would be the end of her world, too. Helpless though she was in many ways, Polly loved her son too much for her to imagine life without him. Slowly Cryssie's hand went to her mouth as she considered that stark possibility, the hell into which she and her sister would descend.

It took about fifteen minutes to reach the fairground, its gaudy sights and ear-splitting sounds as they drew up making Cryssie nearly heave. Milo had always loved this annual treat, but how different it all was when they were here to enjoy themselves, she thought, tears welling up in her eyes.

As they got out of the car, Jed nodded towards the stationary police vehicle waiting there. 'They've beaten us to it,' he said. 'But there's such a crowd here it'll take all of us to cover the place.' He strode in front of her to speak to the officer standing there, and before she could catch him up he turned to face her. 'There's still no news,' he said briefly. He caught her hand. 'Right. We'll start around the outside, where the staff caravans are always parked.'

'I still don't think Milo could have got here by himself,' Cryssie said, the hopelessness in her voice saying it all. 'And it's not like him to do such a thing.' She paused for a moment, holding her side, which was burning with a tense pain. 'Oh, Jed,' she murmured in a desperate whisper. 'I'm…I'm so frightened…'

He stopped in his tracks then, and pulled her towards him, holding her in a tight embrace that comforted her and strengthened her at the same time. 'Hang in there, Cryssie,' he said, his mouth close against her ear. 'We're not done yet, believe me. Don't give up. I *never* give up! Never, never, never!'

Momentarily reassured, Cryssie allowed herself to be almost dragged along as, with Milo's picture in his hand, Jed approached and questioned each and every adult and child they came to, knocking on caravan doors, checking behind trailers. She was caught up in a surreal situation, Cryssie thought, with the rollercoasters and rides careering along their dizzy routes, and everyone screaming in mock terror, with deafening music adding to the din. But *her* terror was real, and it was the worst sensation she'd ever experienced. There were no words that would ever describe it, she thought, her pervading sense of failure in their mission filling her with a strange calm.

And the worst thing was that there were so many small children there—any one of whom could have been Milo. Similar little fair curls, dressed in similar T-shirts… But *they* were all with adults, being held safely by the hand. All enjoying themselves.

They'd almost completed their circuit of the ground when

suddenly, right alongside them, the door to one of the caravans opened and a young girl of about eight or nine stood on the steps, talking over her shoulder to someone behind her. She was clutching a Runaway Rascal in her arms.

'Come on,' the child said. 'Bring yours, and we'll go and ask my dad if we can have a candy floss. Do you like candy floss, Milo?'

MILO! Jed and Cryssie leapt forward at the word, just as Milo—their Milo—followed the girl down the steps of the van. In unison, they both cried out his name, and in the brief seconds that followed gathered him up in their arms in such frantic relief that, afterwards Cryssie couldn't remember a thing about it. In her dizzy euphoria she as good as lost consciousness as she hugged and kissed the child, over and over again. But what she did remember was Jed's reaction. Because he was holding her—and Milo—in a circular embrace that almost robbed her of breath, and when she at last turned her head to look up at him she saw tears—real tears—slipping silently down his face. And witnessing that was so natural that she unselfconsciously kissed his wet cheeks, tasting the salt on her lips.

'Thank God,' was all he said.

Quickly regaining his self-control, he rang Polly. 'Polly? Milo's safe. We're coming home!'

The way he spoke the words filled Cryssie with a deep sense of wonder. *We're coming home!* Would any words ever again match those? she thought.

After letting the police know, and still without asking any questions of Milo, they turned to go back to the car. But the child hesitated.

'This is my new friend,' he said. 'She's called Victoria, and we've been playing with our Runaways in her caravan. I brought mine with me,' he added, holding Jed by the hand and looking up at them as if nothing unusual had happened that afternoon.

'Well, thank you, Victoria, for letting Milo play,' Cryssie said. 'I'm afraid we have to go home now, because Milo's mummy is waiting for him. Perhaps we'll come and see you again soon.'

As they walked slowly back to the car Jed and Cryssie exchanged glances over Milo's head. They both knew that there would be time for explanations later. But for now, blessed thankfulness was the only emotion they felt, or that mattered.

Much later, after the police had gone, they gently persuaded Milo to tell them how he'd got to the fair.

'I went on the bus,' he said importantly. 'And I wasn't going to the fair, anyway.' He helped himself to another potato crisp. 'I was going to see you, Jed, at your house. I wanted to throw stones in the river, like we did before. Cryssie said I couldn't go this time, but I thought you wouldn't mind. There were lots of people and children at the bus stop as I went by, and then a bus came and everyone got on, and I did as well.'

'But—didn't anyone ask you who you were with?' Polly asked. 'Who paid for you?'

Milo shrugged. 'No one. I didn't have any money. No one paid. And then everyone got off, and so did I, and then we were all at the fair. After a bit I saw Victoria—you know, with her Runaway—and she said we could play with them together.' He sucked a finger. 'Her mummy and daddy work the rides,' he said. 'But I didn't see them at all.'

So it was that easy, Cryssie thought, for a child to mingle, to become anonymous, in a crowd. And for no one to realise or notice.

After they'd all had something to eat, and put Milo to bed,

Polly said, 'I feel so utterly exhausted I'm going up as well—if you don't mind, Cryssie—Jed?' she asked. 'I just want this day to end, and never to know another one like it.'

'Of course, Polly,' Jed said gently. 'You'll feel better in the morning. So will we all,' he added.

Polly hesitated. 'I shall feel better when I know what you intend doing about the matter of the scarf I stole, Jed,' she said simply, and Cryssie was touched at her sister's courage to mention this today. 'You must know that I stole from the store?' she went on slowly. 'And—'

'Yes—I was informed,' Jed said. 'But, please think no more about it, Polly. I shan't,' he added. 'That's a very small drop of water in the ocean.' He was silent for a moment, then, 'I was wondering the other day whether you'd be interested in a small part-time job at Latimer's, Polly—as a beauty consultant in the cosmetics department,' he said, not looking at Cryssie, who had raised her eyes at him. 'We stock most top-of-the-range make-up brands, as you probably know, but we've never bothered with a resident expert…someone who could give advice. It would be a very useful asset to us…if you're interested, that is?'

'Oh—Jed…' Polly was overwhelmed at the suggestion.

'You'd obviously need to think it over,' he went on quickly. 'But it would be the sort of arrangement that could easily fit in with Milo's school hours.'

He sat back and looked across at Cryssie then, a tiny glint of triumph in his eyes. How long had he been thinking this one up? she thought. But it was a wonderful possibility, and it might help to restore some of Polly's self esteem—which, as he had so perceptively pointed out, was in short supply.

And, as a first step in that direction, Polly went right over to Jed and kissed him softly on both cheeks. 'I'll let you have my acceptance in writing,' she said.

When Cryssie and Jed were alone together, she said curiously, 'Was your suggestion to Polly a sudden rush of blood to the head, or…?'

'No,' he replied. 'It's been on my mind for a while that a professional in the beauty department, to give advice, would undoubtedly shift more of the expensive brands. And your sister is a very good advertisement, isn't she?'

Cryssie smiled. Polly had always known how to make the best of herself—a talent she could pass on. 'Well, thanks for thinking of that, Jed,' she said slowly. 'It might solve more than one problem for her.'

'That's what I thought,' he said smoothly.

Sitting there, close together on the settee, Cryssie looked up at him thoughtfully. 'I could not have kept going today without you, Jed,' she said.

He ran his hand through his hair restlessly. 'If anyone…if anything had happened to Milo—' he began, then was unable to go on. And Cryssie realised, again, that he loved their little boy almost as much as they did. 'I could do with a drink,' he said. 'You don't feel like going out somewhere, I suppose…?'

'I couldn't face anywhere else today, Jed, but there's a bottle of red wine in the pantry. Let's be devils and drink the lot! It's only nine o'clock,' she said lightly.

She brought out two wine glasses, while Jed uncorked the bottle, and filled them to the brim. Then they stood facing each other in the modest room and sipped at the glowing liquid, their eyes meeting as unspoken messages passed between them.

Presently, Cryssie said, 'Some hours ago—or was it days ago?—I think you said we needed to talk…'

Straight away he put down his glass and took hers from her hand, then pulled her towards him hungrily. Towering above her, with his arms tightly around her, he looked down for a long moment into her green uncomplicated eyes, whose sincerity had captured his heart from the very first moment. 'Your sister has promised to give me her acceptance in writing,' he murmured, kissing her softly behind her ear once, twice, three times. Cryssie felt her desire for him tingle with a burning fire. 'But two words from you now will do. Will you agree to marry me, Cryssie? Please? Will you say yes?'

They stood there as one, immovable in their shared pleasure at being close, at feeling their bodies meld with an intoxicating heat, and Cryssie thought that she wouldn't mind staying there, like that, for eternity! Softly, she said, 'And why should I?'

He took a deep, deep breath. 'Well, mainly because I've promised Milo that he's going to come and live with me one day, but also because I love you,' he said simply. 'I *love* you. That's all.'

That's *all?* But that was all she had ever wanted to hear him say! And at last he had said it! He *did* love her! She looked up at him adoringly. 'I never thought I'd hear you say that,' she whispered. 'I didn't think you were…'

'What? You didn't think I was capable of loving? Thought that my only obsession was chasing the material world?' He smiled a tight, grim smile. 'My ex-wife obviously thought that, too,' he said. 'That's why, very soon after our marriage, she insisted on separate bedrooms—and a separate credit card account—which I readily agreed to. Until I discovered what she wanted a disproportionate amount of my money for.' He paused, his lingering resentment still obvious. 'She insisted that she wanted cosmetic surgery and breast enhancements…as if nature hadn't already endowed her with more than her fair share! Just to keep up with her empty-headed friends. That's when I put a stop to it all. And she never wanted children—something she told me *after* our wedding day. Because she'd never recover her figure, so she said.'

Hearing him tell her all this made Cryssie hold him even more tightly. He had been so deeply hurt, so let down, she thought. No wonder he sometimes showed a hard, unfeeling edge.

Gently, she took him by the hand and led him upstairs to her bedroom, shutting the door behind them quietly. Totally unselfconsciously, he stepped out of his clothes, dropping them carelessly to the floor, and they lay down on the bed together, Jed cradling her in his arms.

Dreamily, she said, 'I hereby formally agree to stay with you, in your bed, at your side, satisfying your every whim, until my final breath. Will that do?'

Raising himself on one elbow, he looked down at her for a long, heart-throbbing moment, then slowly he began to undress her, until she, too, was completely naked. His strong, warm hands caressing her body made her gasp in anticipation and sexual excitement, his eyes—those dark pools of passionate promise—mesmerising her as they always did. Then his mouth came down on hers greedily, and the moist meeting of their parted lips was a mere prelude to the ecstasy that was to come. There was no sense of urgency as they lay there, locked together, and Cryssie knew instinctively that he would take time to bring her to that indescribable point of fulfilled desire.

'There *is* one more thing I need,' he said softly, gazing down at her, drinking in the soft contours of her body, the smoothness of her flat stomach and rounded thighs. 'Will you promise that we'll give Milo at least four cousins to ruin the grass at Shepherd's Keep?'

'Only four?' she teased.

'Well, for starters,' he said. 'But, given that I'll always be needing your business acumen, it might mean we'll have to employ a couple of nannies!'

'Then I shall consider my part in it a formal obligation,' Cryssie said, 'so that the Hunter dynasty will continue to thrive for many years to come!'

She nestled into him, loving the musky, manly smell of him, the pulsating strength of his chest against the softness of her bare breasts. Then a little smile played across her lips for a second, and he murmured, 'What's funny?'

'I was just thinking that everything that's happened to us—to Polly and to Milo and to me—is all because of television's *Runaway Rascals!* Isn't that bizarre?' She traced Jed's lips and jaw with her forefinger, which he quickly took in his mouth and held between his teeth. 'If I hadn't bumped into you on Christmas Eve—when I was trying to buy one of them—you'd never have noticed me at all. I'd have been just one of the insignificant members of staff at Hydebound you'd have ditched, along with everyone else, without another thought.'

'I suppose that is possible,' he admitted. 'Though something tells me that Crystal Rowe wouldn't have remained anonymous for long!'

She smiled again, smugly. 'And even though you selfishly insisted on taking the last four of those dolls—I called you a few names, I can tell you, one of your shop assistants actually found one after all! And brought it to me—here!'

'Of course she did,' he said smoothly.

Cryssie frowned. 'What do you mean by that?'

He smiled that slow, superior, heart-stopping smile. 'Oh…it's just that yours was one of the four I'd bought, but found I didn't need after all. So the assistant and I hatched a plan for you—for Milo—not to be disappointed.'

'Well, of all the…' For once, Cryssie was speechless. Then,

after a second or two, she said, 'So, Mr Have-It-All-Your-Own-Way, is there *any* plan of yours that is never fulfilled?'

'Never,' he breathed softly into her ear. 'Allow me to demonstrate…'

* * * * *

Brad shoved the truck into gear and drove to the bottom of the hill, where the road forked. Turn left, and he'd be home in five minutes. Turn right, and he was headed for Indian Rock.

He had no damn business going to Indian Rock.

He had nothing to say to Meg McKettrick, and if he never set eyes on the woman again, it would be two weeks too soon.

He turned right.

He couldn't have said why.

He just drove straight to the Dixie Dog Drive-In.

Back in the day, he and Meg used to meet at the Dixie Dog, by tacit agreement, when either of them had been away. It had been some kind of universe thing, purely intuitive.

Passing familiar landmarks, Brad told himself he ought to turn around. The old days were gone. Things had ended badly between him and Meg anyhow, and she wasn't going to be at the Dixie Dog.

He kept driving.

He rounded a bend, and there was the Dixie Dog. Its big neon sign, a giant hot dog, was all lit up and going through its corny sequence—first it was covered in red squiggles of light, meant to suggest ketchup, and then yellow, for mustard.

Brad pulled into one of the slots next to a speaker, rolled down the truck window and ordered.

A girl roller-skated out with the order about five minutes later.

When she wheeled up to the driver's window, smiling, her eyes went wide with recognition, and she dropped the tray with a clatter.

Silently Brad swore. Damn if he hadn't forgotten he was a famous country singer.

The girl, a skinny thing wearing too much eye makeup, immediately started to cry. "I'm sorry!" she sobbed, squatting to gather up the mess.

"It's okay," Brad answered quietly, leaning to look down at her, catching a glimpse of her plastic name tag. "It's okay, Mandy. No harm done."

"I'll get you another dog and a shake right away, Mr. O'Ballivan!"

"Mandy?"

She stared up at him pitifully, sniffling. Thanks to the copious tears, most of the goop on her eyes had slid south. "Yes?"

"When you go back inside, could you not mention seeing me?"

"But you're Brad O'Ballivan!"

"Yeah," he answered, suppressing a sigh. "I know."

She rolled a little closer. "You wouldn't happen to have a picture you could autograph for me, would you?"

"Not with me," Brad answered.

"You could sign this napkin, though," Mandy said. "It's only got a little chocolate on the corner."

Brad took the paper napkin and her order pen, and scrawled his name. Handed both items back through the window.

She turned and whizzed back toward the side entrance to the Dixie Dog.

Brad waited, marveling that he hadn't considered incidents like this one before he'd decided to come back home. In retrospect, it seemed shortsighted, to say the least, but the truth was, he'd expected to be—Brad O'Ballivan.

Presently Mandy skated back out again, and this time she managed to hold on to the tray.

"I didn't tell a soul!" she whispered. "But Heather and Darlene *both* asked me why my mascara was all smeared." Efficiently she hooked the tray onto the bottom edge of the window.

Brad extended payment, but Mandy shook her head.

"The boss said it's on the house, since I dumped your first order on the ground."

He smiled. "Okay, then. Thanks."

Mandy retreated, and Brad was just reaching for the food when a bright red Blazer whipped into the space beside his. The driver's door sprang open, crashing into the metal speaker, and somebody got out in a hurry.

Something quickened inside Brad.

And in the next moment Meg McKettrick was standing practically on his running board, her blue eyes blazing.

Brad grinned. "I guess you're not over me after all," he said.

ITALIAN BOSS, HOUSEKEEPER BRIDE
by Sharon Kendrick

Book #2687

THE ITALIAN BILLIONAIRE'S CHRISTMAS MIRACLE
by *Catherine Spencer*

Book #: 2688

Domenico Silvaggio d'Avalos knows that beautiful,
unworldly Arlene Russell isn't mistress material—
but might she be suitable as his wife?

HIS CHRISTMAS BRIDE
by *Helen Brooks*

Book #: 2689

Powerful billionaire Zak Hamilton understood
Blossom's vulnerabilities, and he had to have her.
What was more, he'd make sure he claimed her
as his bride—by Christmas!

Be sure not to miss out on these two fabulous
Christmas stories available December 2007,
brought to you by Harlequin Presents!

REQUEST YOUR FREE BOOKS!

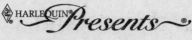

2 FREE NOVELS PLUS 2 FREE GIFTS!

YES! Please send me 2 FREE Harlequin Presents® novels and my 2 FREE gifts. After receiving them, if I don't wish to receive any more books, I can return the shipping statement marked "cancel." If I don't cancel, I will receive 6 brand-new novels every month and be billed just $3.80 per book in the U.S., or $4.47 per book in Canada, plus 25¢ shipping and handling per book and applicable taxes, if any*. That's a savings of close to 15% off the cover price! I understand that accepting the 2 free books and gifts places me under no obligation to buy anything. I can always return a shipment and cancel at any time. Even if I never buy another book from Harlequin, the two free books and gifts are mine to keep forever.

106 HDN EEXK 306 HDN EEXV

Name	(PLEASE PRINT)	
Address		Apt. #
City	State/Prov.	Zip/Postal Code

Signature (if under 18, a parent or guardian must sign)

Mail to the **Harlequin Reader Service®**:
IN U.S.A.: P.O. Box 1867, Buffalo, NY 14240-1867
IN CANADA: P.O. Box 609, Fort Erie, Ontario L2A 5X3

Not valid to current Harlequin Presents subscribers.

Want to try two free books from another line?
Call 1-800-873-8635 or visit www.morefreebooks.com.

* Terms and prices subject to change without notice. NY residents add applicable sales tax. Canadian residents will be charged applicable provincial taxes and GST. This offer is limited to one order per household. All orders subject to approval. Credit or debit balances in a customer's account(s) may be offset by any other outstanding balance owed by or to the customer. Please allow 4 to 6 weeks for delivery.

Your Privacy: Harlequin is committed to protecting your privacy. Our Privacy Policy is available online at www.eHarlequin.com or upon request from the Reader Service. From time to time we make our lists of customers available to reputable firms who may have a product or service of interest to you. If you would prefer we not share your name and address, please check here. ☐

HP07

I ♥ HARLEQUIN Presents

**BROUGHT TO YOU BY FANS OF
HARLEQUIN PRESENTS.**

We are its editors and authors
and biggest fans—and we'd
love to hear from YOU!

Subscribe today to our online blog at
www.iheartpresents.com

HARLEQUIN *Presents*®

THE ROYAL HOUSE OF NIROLI
Always passionate, always proud.

**The richest royal family in the world—
a family united by blood and passion,
torn apart by deceit and desire.**

By royal decree, Harlequin Presents is delighted to bring you
The Royal House of Niroli. Step into the glamorous, enticing
world of the Nirolian Royal Family. As the king ails he
must find an heir…each month an exciting new installment
follows the epic search for the true Nirolian king. Eight heirs,
eight passionate romances, eight fantastic stories!

Coming in December:

THE PRINCE'S FORBIDDEN VIRGIN
by Robyn Donald
Book #2683

**Although Rosa Fierezza knows he's forbidden fruit,
she's under Max's spell. However, just when Rosa and
Max give up all hope of being together, the truth about
a scandal from the past may set them free….**

*Be sure not to miss the next book
in this fabulous series!*

Coming in January:
BRIDE BY ROYAL APPOINTMENT
by Raye Morgan Book #2691

www.eHarlequin.com

Silhouette

SPECIAL EDITION™

**brings you a heartwarming
new McKettrick's story from**

NEW YORK TIMES BESTSELLING AUTHOR

LINDA LAEL MILLER

THE McKETTRICK
Way

Meg McKettrick is surprised to be reunited
with her high school flame, Brad O'Ballivan,
who has returned home to his family's
neighboring ranch. After seeing Meg again,
Brad realizes he still loves her. But the pride
of both manage to interfere with love...until
an unexpected matchmaker gets involved.

—— McKettrick Women ——

Available December wherever you buy books.